My name is:

_____

Write your name here:

Christmas Wings for Brian

A heartwarming story of a little boy from Wilkes-Barre PA, whose shoulders kept growing

This story begins with a nineteen-month-old named Brian, who then grows up to be a special young man with special gifts above all others. His love of Christmas trains was only surpassed by his love of planes and all air vehicles. Superman had become his favorite airplane. Every year after Christmas, he saw the huge tree and everything else disappear. He would go to bed and when he would awaken, everything would be gone—the tree, the train, all the toys, the helicopters, the big and small panes at the tree platform airport. Worse than that, even the platform where everything was displayed was gone. But, the next year, it was back.

Christmas was a great day every year and it stayed that way for days after so much so that it seemed like it would never end each and every year. After it was about to all go away at the end of just his second Christmas season, after a few days passed with all platform items gone, he got over it. That year, mom and dad took him for a special visit to a Christmas wizard who was also an angel. The wizard had a huge platform with trains and flying objects even though it was a few weeks after Christmas. It was before Brian had even turned two-years old. In this visit, he picked up more real information that a child his age should have been able to handle… Yet, he was able to manage the truth well, for over five years.

Then, in his seventh year, when he reached the age of reason, he finally had figured out the Christmas mystery. No matter what, no longer was there any sadness at the end of the Christmas season. This year, like every other year, he was ready for it all to go away but the Christmas angel had told him "Fear Not!" No longer did he care about going to sleep one particular night after Christmas, and poof, the morning would present a big void. It was his year

Just like he knew it would; it happened. This time, there was not an icicle or even a tiny piece of platform snow anywhere to make him think it was not just a silly dream—like how it was explained every other year. This year mom and dad knew that Brian knew the secret and he promised them he would not tell his younger brother and sister. Brian had grown; still loved Christmas; but was changed by the visit with the angel and this was the big year.

On his seventh birthday, when he woke up, he got a big surprise. He did not know what it was all about but he had been assured that it would be good. For five years he had felt the muscular nubs in his back. A wizard had made a great prediction that the muscles in his back that seemed to be outgrowths of the scapula, could support huge wings. This discovery over time would become the most significant thing that would happen in Brian's life until the day his gifts were full grown. His story is what this book is all about.

This is great family reading. A real family is highlighted in this fine uplifting story. Thank you for reading it. You can read this book to all your children and their friends and they will love it. Enjoy! Have a great and magical day. I have a feeling that the tree, the toys, and the toot-toot and perhaps even more, will all be back next year if not sooner.

BRIAN W. KELLY

Published by: LETS GO PUBLISH!   LETS
Publisher   Brian P. Kelly   GO
Email: info@letsgopublish.com   PUBLISH
Web site   www.letsgopublish.com

Library of Congress Copyright Information Pending
Book Cover Design by Brian W. Kelly
Editor—   Brian P. Kelly

ISBN Information: The International Standard Book Number (ISBN) is a
unique machine-readable identification number, which marks any book
unmistakably. The ISBN is the clear standard in the book industry. 159
countries and territories are officially ISBN members. The Official ISBN
For this book is on the outside cover: **ISBN 978-1-951562-02-1**

The price for this work is: **$11.95 USD**
10   9   8   7   6   5   4   3   2   1
Release Date: October 2019

Publisher's Note: *Please check out www.letsgopublish.com to read the
latest version of our heartfelt acknowledgments updated for this book. On
the site, please click the bottom item of the main menu!*
Other books are available at amazon.com/author/brianwkelly

Dedication

Table of Contents

Chapter 1 The People in this Exciting Christmas Story

The Katille home -- 54 Cummings Street, Ashley PA 18702

Brian is now 39 years old and his secret is still safe. He agreed to write his story, and his Mom, my wife, Patricia offered to take the shorthand and then type up the whole book for the family. Thanks Mom. This book has been in progress from when mom started typing it on an old IBM PC in 1982 and she kept at it off and on for years until now, when she and Brian finished it.

I am the dad, Brian "Brunick" Katille. My brothers and sisters are Nancy, Eddie, Mary and Joe (these last two are twins). Pat and I have three children: Brian, Mortrock, and Katers. On the humorous side, when Katers was able to talk well, one of the first things she wanted was to change our last name from Katille pronounced (ka-teel) to Karpathiokatee, pronounced (Car-Pay-Thee-Oh-Kah-Tee). When I found out it would cost the family $230.00 at City Hall, I nixed that idea very quickly. OK, Brian wants to talk now. It's his show so here goes:

Brian: The picture on the prior page before my dad went through his little diatribe (OK, I liked it too) shows where our family lived–54 Cummings Street. We really lived in the daytime at 60 Cummings Street, which was right next door on the left. That's where my best friend, Mary Zabola lived. We all slept at 54 Cummings so we could enjoy mom's panapoona (our name for pancakes) every morning.

The picture on page 1 shows the house when it was remodeled right before the magic in 1987. Don't ask me where they got this picture because cell phones were not invented then—I think.

Below is an ad for a Theatre in our hometown.

I told Mom to put the *A Christmas Carol* ad up there above this text because it makes the book pages look better. I love Scrooge after he becomes the good Scrooge.

It is my favorite story except this one which I am now telling.

Besides my best buddy Mary, there were the other Zabolas—Dawn, Kim and David. They also lived there with their mom, Barbie and dad, Big Joe. We were over their house a lot when we were growing up.

There was always something good on the stove and even on days that we did not plan to go there, the great smells from their kitchen window pulled us over. My mom says Barbie was a great cook and loved to share.

By the way, though there were three of us kids and mom and Dad, we had just two bedrooms for most of the time when we were growing up. There was a time that the three of us slept in the same double bed. When she moved from her crib, Katers was in the middle and always warm between her two older brothers When I got bigger, dad and Uncle Walter and Uncle Robert and Uncle Marty built a new bedroom for me and they built a recreation room beneath it. We called it the Sun Room because of the big window. It was where the big swing had been outside.

When it was finished, I had it made. It was great. It had a big wall mirror so I could watch the muscles growing on my back without my brother and sister seeing me.

As Mortrock and Katers got bigger, it was logical for Mortrock to come and move into my bedroom. Before that happened, at first Mortrock slept in a used bed mom and dad got at the Sallies. At the time, we could not afford a bunk bed or trundle bed.

Even before that, the neighbors had given mom and dad a different double bed but with our jumping up and down on it, the springs broke. Dad had figured out how to get the two beds into their bedroom so that their heads were against the wall and the bottoms of the beds were about a foot apart.

So, for a few years before Mortrock moved in with me, He and Katers could go through the secret passageway between the beds and get in on either side. They loved that and talked about it all the time like it was a big adventure.

I was ok with my single bed in my little room except when I heard Mortrock and Katers laughing when we were supposed to get to sleep, I did miss the days when we were all together. In a few years, it would be me and Mortdock again. Katers room was right by mom & dad's so she was never scared.

The Katille home and the Zabola home were both at the top of the hill on Cummings Street. If we went left or right from these homes, the hills were steep. As kids, our big wheels came in very handy. It was a long haul back up the hills, after the great ride down, however, Now as I think back, it was dangerous—but nobody ever got hurt.

I'm not only the person telling everybody who reads this the big story about Brian P. Katille. Right now, I am also your narrator, Brian Patrick Katille and

I am happy to meet you all. I am also the major
character in this story. I am a lot older now (39) than
when this story happened on Cummings Street in our
hometown at the time of Ashley, PA.

I have the distinct pleasure of telling this
phenomenally incredible story about me. My brother
Mortrock and my sister Katers and a bunch of other
wonderful people have small roles in the story but they
all had big roles in my wonderful life. I can't believe I
already have over four pages finished already, including
Da's stuff in the beginning.

The facts in this story come mostly from me but
Morty and Katers (sometimes called Katie) also
provided a lot of insights about what was going on at our
Cummings Street residence. Mom filled in a lot with
stuff from the younger age stuff as well as the visits to
the Pops and the Nanas.

Mom, so you see it I am going to say some of this
stuff again so you will be mentioned more than once.
Ahem…some other facts and stories recalled come from
my mom—Patricia Trosk Katille, my dad—Brian W.
Katille, and my grandparents: Grand-Pop— "Smokey"
Trosk; Nana—Arlene "Skippo" Trosk; Grand Pop—
Edward J. Katille; and Nana—Irene "Grandma Biddie"
Katilles.

Because I still have this great gift of flight, which I
have yet to introduce, much of this story is depicted as
true though I cannot add any truth to the notion of my
special gift as it is a spiritual secret. I will tell what I
can. I was told once by somebody who I do not remember

that this story is also a government secret. It can't be though or you would not be able to read it to your kids.

I do add a few extra facts of my own and a few fake stories (but not many) as, after all, I am the main character in the story. But, first of course, I had to be born. Others in the story are uncle Joseph Katille and aunt Diane Katille; Uncle Bill Daniels and aunt Mary Daniels. Of course there is also my dad's big brother, uncle Ed "Eudart" Katille, and his big sister, aunt Nancy Flanders.

I can't wait to tell you this whole story.

In case you missed it, which I don't think you will—the Katille's and the Trosks were big Christmas people. We still are.

By the way, that big three story house on the first page was really, really big. It had two bathrooms and eventually it had three bedrooms and a big sunroom. It was a gift from God that my uncles were able to help Dad and Pop Trosk build my new bedroom. What a great place to live and most importantly for us kids—to play.

Before I was born, my mom and dad lived in the one finished bedroom in the house. There was a second bedroom but it took my being born before Dad ever made it nice enough to be the second bedroom.

There were three rooms downstairs—living room, dining room and kitchen plus a pantry with a sink and a full bath off the kitchen. Oh, and yes, there was a bath upstairs for Mom and dad and we three kids when we eventually came into the fold.

Grandpop Edward J Katille, also known as Pop K, lived down the street at 18 Cummings Street. When dad and mom bought the big house on Cummings Street in 1975, it cost them $21,000 but it needed a lot of work. Pop Katille, living right down the street at 18 Cummings Street did most of that work.

I remember none of it as all that work was done well before I was born, My grandparents on mom's side, aka "The Trosks" lived on Hillside Street right next door to mom's Brother Marty and his beautiful wife Cathy, and their three Martin Trosk Kids – Martin Jr., Scott, and Erin. What a nice and wonderful family.

Pop Katille promised my dad, his son, Brian W. Katille, that he would do whatever was needed to fix up the house on the inside. There were some holes in the walls and ceilings plus the whole place—all rooms (three downstairs plus pantry & b-room, and two upstairs (plus one bath) needed to be repaired and repainted and there were a few little holes in the wall that needed some patches.

Pop Katille decided that as soon as my mom and dad came back from their honeymoon, he would get started on the job. No, I was not there yet. So, while they were gone, Pop went to Main Hardware and got all of the supplies that he would need.

I, Brian P. Katille am the first-born child of Brian and Patricia Katille. I made my first appearance on May

28, 1980. I'll tell you all about that after a few more chapters. I'll even show you some pictures. Then, you may have to look up in the sky to find out what happened next. Shhh!

For now, let me say that on the day I was born, it was a very nice warm day in our hometown in Pennsylvania. The "stork" did not have to navigate through bad weather like for my brother (December) and my sister (November) The summer was about to come, and it would be a hot one.

My mom and dad had a pool and they needed it with me continually squawking in the shade of the back porch roof on Cummings Street.

About nineteen months later on December 30, 1981, right after Christmas and before New Years Eve, my brother Mortrock was born. I had just had my second Christmas but, at 19 months old, I do think I knew a lot about what was happening. I do remember everything about Mr. Christian's visit which we'll tell you about soon.

The neighbors called Mortrock and I *Irish twins*. Cold as it might have been on December 31, it was a warm day for dad and mom --and their new nineteen month-old-son —me. A few days later, Mom and Dad took Mortrock home to 54 Cummings Street and I loved it until he toughened up. I loved my new brother Mortrock.

My sister Katers waited longer to be born but I am glad she finally appeared almost three years later on

November 12, 1984. She was a beauty as I recall and my mom and dad were thrilled to have a baby girl.

Let me show you a picture of the three Katille kids some time around 1987, the year big things in this story happened to me. This picture was taken at Pop Catille's house at 18 Cummings Street.

From left to right, Me—Brian, Dad, Mortrock, Mom, & little Katers

My dad, Brian Sr. still is a jokester. He chortled about having Irish twins right after Mortrock was born. He said that if the Katille's had the good fortune to have triplets, he would have named the third baby Jesus— pronounced Hey Zeus and he might have named the other two, Joseph and Mary.

But, Katers came when both Mortrock and I were buzzing around the house and both of us could make it up and down the steps.

For the record, mom did not find Dad's jokes amusing at all. Our family was always very religious and my dad loved the idea of Jesus, Mary & Joseph being born in his family.

However, mom had a tough time thinking about real triplets. I guess Mortrock and I were a lot of work, but we always knew we were well loved.

Life was especially good for our family. Dad got a great job with IBM and after a few years, he was making a good salary. Mom was a teacher by trade when Mortrock and I came so quickly after no children for five years. Mom sacrificed to stay home and she helped us all grow up. Mom and dad decided that mom would stay at home to make sure all of us kids grew up right.

As I said, Grandpop and Grandma Katille lived right down the street. Additionally, with the Zabola's right next door on the left and with the Trosks from Hillside Stree, up the house all the time, the families became best friends. Mary Z and I were the same age but Dawn Z was never far away from us when we played.

Mom and Dad originally planned to stay on Cummings Street for a lot of years and then move to a single home. But there were too many good reasons to stay a lot longer. Our family lived on Cummings for thirteen great years. I think I lived there eight years.

Mom and dad had bought the Cummings Street home in 1975 right before they got married. Rather than pay rent, Pop Katille fixed up all the rooms so everybody who should live there had the room. It was a nice place and Pop Katille made it lots nicer. Pop Trosk always liked to tell us when we were growing up that any plumbing problems that Pop Katille encountered, he and his buddy Dehaut fixed them all lickety split.

Pop Katille lived right down the street so he also fixed up the big problems with the unfinished rooms. Because of his work and the work of Pop Trosk and the uncles, it was very good for all of us. Mom and dad wished the home was bigger so they could rent out parts to put more wheaties in our bowls, but we all did fine. And it was not too long before dad's salary made it so life was even better.

All of the members of the family were healthy as were the Zabolas next door. That's all that really mattered to the Katilles.

When I was born and then when Mortrock and Katers came along, we had a big enough house to have a place to sleep. I explained this earlier in this chapter. The side by side beds were occupied by Mortrock and Katers and I had my own big room with a big mirror, that helped me observe the growth of my gift from God. Eventually Mortrock moved in with me.

When we three kids were all born, Katers and Mortrock shared the second bedroom and I got the new smaller bedroom that the Uncles and my grandpops built.

There was never a lot of money to be found even though Dad worked for IBM. Mom and dad bought a couple dressers and the right beds to make sure we all did well in our nice home on 54 Cummings Street.

Here is what the downstairs looked like.

When mom and dad got back from their honeymoon and dad was finally OK, he went back to work at IBM and mom went back to work at the Bureau for the Visually Handicapped.

Pop Katille religiously came up from 18 Cummings Street to our house every morning and he worked 'til about 2:00 pm before he left for home. He really did a lot of work. We were so lucky.

The two rooms upstairs and three + downstairs needed a ton of paint. He patched the holes in the plaster and painted and painted and painted. My dad learned how to do wall-papering and he papered all but the ceiling in the kitchen. Pop Katille patched the ceilings and painted them white. He also patched the walls so dad could wallpaper them. I wish I were old enough at the time to have watched my dad and my grandpas at work. But, the results were outstanding.

The wallpaper dad used in the kitchen was very patriotic--red white and blue with sayings from the

American Revolution. I remember it was very upbeat. Pop also painted the background for the kitchen stove black as well as the stovepipes. He made it real nice.

He also used a special black material to bring back the color from the Wilkes-Barre coal stove we had in the kitchen. Here is a cut out picture of the back door to show how dad painted the new duct work black to match the black kitchen stove that was off to the right.

Take a look on the next page and you will see one of the only other pictures of the kitchen I could find that has that special wall-paper. That's me below in 1982 with my three-month-old brother Mortrock on top of the trestle table that Uncle Bucko Grimes made for our family..

Mom worked hard in the kitchen lining the cupboards with special sticky paper after Pop had painted the outside and the inside of the cupboards. She made it real nice as I recall.

To go with the patriotic theme, Pop painted the kitchen door and the cellar door and the wainscoating an antique red color that matched the wallpaper.

Everybody loved the look of the kitchen.

Coming in the front door, Dad wallpapered the entire left side of the house. With the open staircase the wall went all the way up to the second-floor ceiling.

Dad papered the other side of the hallway upstairs also from the front bedroom to the bathroom in the rear. He also papered one wall a few years later in what became my new room and it was beautiful.

The last wall that he papered was downstairs in the dining room. It was tropical flowery and matched the green rug that mom bought for that room.

Pop patched and painted all of the walls that were not painted a nice shade of white. He painted one wall in Mortrock & Katers' room pink and it matched the rug that we got for that room.

Eventually pop was done and mom and dad fully moved in about four years before I was born. It took Pop Katille about five months to finish all the work before the move-in. Technically it was not a full move-in as mom and dad lived in whatever room was not being worked on until it was all ready.

Cummings Street was a great place to live. Let me go back in time now to the period in which Mom and Dad had just gotten married after buying the modest house on Cummings Street. It is a great story about how life together began for mom and dad. It is the unique story of their honeymoon. Only Hollywood in the days of John Wayne movies could top this story. I hope you like it.

Chapter 2 Mom and Dad's Honeymoon!

I heard this story a thousand times and I like hearing it every time. Mom and Dad came back from the honeymoon at Mount Airy Lodge early because dad got hurt doing the organized athletics at the resort. Below is a nice postcard of the resort.

Dad told me that on the second day of the Honeymoon, Monday, they played tennis, then they played softball, and then in the afternoon, they went for a long horseback ride with a group. There is a picture at the resort that Mom showed me with dad's head bent over like his chin was in his chest. He said he could not move his head or neck. He looked like he was in pain because he was.

Dad said he was not sure what was wrong but expected to feel better soon. There was a picture taken when Dad and Mom were getting ready to go in for their evening meal. You could see dad's head tilted downwards. I could not find that picture for this story.

When mom and dad got to the table after the athletic day, they were with the same group of friends from the night before. Mom told them that dad was a little sore and Dad did his best to show no pain. He said the red wine at dinner really helped him.

The dinner was delicious, both mom and Dad agreed. They had steak and scallops and a great chocolate cake with thick icing for dessert. After dinner, they had a few cocktails with their new friends and then everybody decided to cash it in for the night.

Dad was getting a bit stiffer and the pain was increasing as he walked the lengthy halls back to the room. The bed was comfortable, but Dad's neck was really hurting.

At Midnight, the pain got so bad the hotel security, Mount Airy Lodge, at mom's request called an ambulance and they took Dad to the Monroe County General Hospital Emergency room. That's the part of the story where everybody normally has a big laugh.

The hospital took X-rays and saw that nothing was broken. They told dad in a few days the inflammation would die down and he would feel much better.

Dad set his watch for 48 hours. He counted the hours. Dad and mom went back to the hotel and Dad finally got to sleep. They gave Dad some strong pills, but he says even today that the pills did nothing that first night.

As we discussed, mom and dad met some nice people the first day and when they went to dinner the second day after dad hurt himself, as noted above, they sat with the same people. The hotel had made table assignments and every day. They were the same.

When Dad hurt himself on Monday, after he went to dinner, and the hospital, he could no longer get out of bed. That was it for dad for meeting people for dinner. Dad said he was in pain all week long even after the 48 hours and it hurt just to move.

I remember hearing dad tell the story lots of times but when mom told it, it took a lot longer and she made it seem funny. Whenever they got to the part where on their honeymoon, dad was not allowed to move from Tuesday through Thursday *on his honeymoon,* the people listening always enjoyed that no matter who told the story—they always had one heck of a belly laugh.

Even Uncle Joe and Uncle Ed who heard the account a number of times over the years, could not hold in their laughter. Dad always seemed to know the big laugh was coming at the same spot in the story, so he got used to it and it did not seem to bother him so much.

Mom says that it really did bother him a lot, but he would sound like a wuss if he complained. She loved making the story go longer to get dad's goat.

Dad said she made things up over the years. I am not sure who I believe. I did not think the story was really funny. Over the years, the story became easier for dad to tell but mom would always cut him off to make sure every detail was covered.

Dad said mom was very nice while he lay incapacitated in their huge King-Size bed at Mount Airy Resort in the Poconos. She said the bed had a big mirror on the ceiling and this bugged dad as he got to see how much in pain he actually was.

Dad said there were three bright spots for him every day. Breakfast, Lunch, and Dinner. Then he would say "That's It! That's all there was—even the TV stations were lousy."

If he thought mom would go for it, dad told me he might have asked for a late-night snack, but he knew he was a burden. Having mom with him for meals was punishment enough for her as dad would say. "Honeymoons were meant to be fun for both parties."

Mom was glad that she had met other couples and after Tuesday's lunch, she stayed with them at their invitation for their recreation events. They also saved a spot for her at all their meals.

They were all very nice and took mom wherever they were going, and she appreciated it. There was a lot to do but her partner, my dad, was down so she could not play in everything.

It did give her some of what she was missing from Dad being hurt and all. Because mom had begun to make do and if the truth be known, was actually beginning to have some fun, dad's meals got delivered later and later.

Mom enjoyed eating with the group of new friends. Dad said he did not mind but then again, he talked about it a lot like as if Mom was enjoying herself while he was not having any fun at all. He could not have been having fun.

Getting through Tuesday seemed like an eternity. Dad said he expected to feel better by the end of the day or perhaps the next, but he did not feel better.

Mom was not there for him to even complain to. He said often when recounting the Honeymoon, that even the TV shows were lousy and the pain made it hard to sleep. So, overall, it was pretty boring and miserable for Dad.

Wondering when dad would be OK had to make it very unpleasant for Mom too so neither of them were having a picnic. By the end of Tuesday dad felt worse. When Mom came with dinner at about 8:00PM it was cold but that was OK for dad.

He was glad mom was enjoying herself, really, and he felt he would be joining her soon. It did not happen.

The friends were going to a concert at the resort so mom went with them that night and again dad watched prime time TV. He hoped he would fall asleep and wake up better but there was little relief even the next day. Each day was the same.

On Friday when dad got up, he realized that on the coming Sunday they would be checking out and he was hoping Mom might agree to depart from the honeymoon early as he was still bedridden. He hoped to watch the weekend football games on his own TV at home.

Heading home

Dad could not drive because he could not keep his head upright for any length of time. He said it was like having an anvil for a head.

Dad's Volkswagen Bus was a stick shift and mom had never driven it. She called Uncle Joe who kindly agreed to come up to the Poconos by early afternoon on Friday to pick the two honeymooners up from their week of "fun."

It was about an hour ride from home. The shock absorbers on the "bus" were not so great nor was the condition of the roads and so dad felt every bump on the way home.

Dad knew that's how it would be, and he was not looking forward to the ride home. When Uncle Joe got there, Mom and the security team were able to get dad into the Volkswagen bus and they helped him lie down on the floor with a big pillow. Mom drove uncle Joe's car home and followed the "bus." It took about an hour, they said.

There were no cell phones back then so there was no talking between mom and uncle Joe on the way home. Before mom had called Joe that morning, she called Joshy Bohunk, a good friend. Mom and dad had just closed the mortgage on the house and nobody had lived in the home even one night before the honeymoon. There were no beds anyway.

While on the honeymoon, the bed arrived thankfully, and Pop Kells let the delivery people in When she called him, Mom asked Joshy Bohunk if he would assemble the bed and put the springs and mattress on it as dad could not lift anything.

Somehow dad says when he got into the house and up the stairs, the bed was all set up and somebody (*God love them*—dad's words) had put a sheet etc. on the new bed so all dad had to do was climb in.

He said he was a lot better--about 75% OK when he got into the bed. On that day, he does not remember much after that.

He fell asleep. He was home. He was a little better the next day and after about three more days, dad said he was functional with just a couple twinges of pain every now and then. He got some stronger medicine from Doctor Decker when he got home.

Uncle Franny Kurilla, his great friend had already carried the new refrigerator up the front steps of the house. Lots of steps. When Joshy Bohumk and uncle Joe got dad up the steps, they filled that refrigerator up with beer.

Mom and dad had not even gotten their first food order. Dad said that the beer plus a few nips of VO made everything else better until he was all better. The weekend football games made time go much faster.

On Monday, one week after hurting himself, Dad finally was able to move around. He went to the grocery store and bought a few things and for my mom and dad, their life together was about to begin.

Though the people at Mount Airy were nice and they did give a partial refund, mom and dad never ever got that honeymoon in the Poconos that they had planned for so long.

Maybe it is on their bucket list!

Chapter 3 Breezie, Our First Doggie!

Hello Doggy

My Aunt, Mary Daniels, had two beautiful dogs. One was named Burf, and the other was named Muggles. My dad called Muggles **_Bagel Wagel_**. Both of the dogs were female. Dad loved them both.

Burf was the only puppy in a litter from *Mrs. Beasely*, my Aunt Nancy's dog. The other partner in all of these dog entanglements that produced offspring was a guy the family respectfully called "visitor."

Burf found her own visitor and she had a litter of beautiful puppies. When just two puppies were left, Aunt Mary, who knew my dad wanted a dog for their new family, brought two little five-week old rascals over to the Cummings Street residence.

Dad says he still remembers it like it was yesterday. He and mom were in the kitchen. The two puppies were sleepy tired but when my mom, Pat came into the room, dad said the little fur-balls came to life.

Mary set both puppies down on the kitchen floor and immediately the one who would be our puppy went to mom's feet and he laid down right on top of them and he just stayed there.

Dad was hoping mom would say that we could keep him. Mom was so taken back by the loving little guy she said yes even before she picked him up.

The other guy was cute too, but mom's heart was taken. Aunt Mary asked Aunt Nancy about the other puppy and she took him and called him Toby.

Mom decided to call our puppy Breezie. He had a name even before he lived with us. Mary said he needed another week or two more with his mom Burf who was feeding him before she could bring him to the house for good. Dad was very excited.

The day came. The little guy was not trained so there were a lot of calls to go on the paper and there was a lot of poop for the first few months of the little guy's life.

Mom and dad could not sleep with the little guy yelping at night so at some point they would take him to one of the rooms that were not in a construction zone. . Pop was working on two rooms at a time so he was the first to greet Breezie every day about 7:00 AM.

Mom and dad were able to sleep, and pop made sure the little guy ate early in the morning when he arrived. Mom and dad went to work and when they came home the doggie joined them.

There were a lot of wet floors and stinky material on the floors in various rooms during this training period. It seemed to last forever but mom and dad were in their twenties and were able to handle it well.

Big fear: Is Breezie going to die?

One morning when Pop Katille came to work on one of the rooms in the house, Breezie was listless and all sweaty looking. I am not sure where they were sleeping then but Pop found mom as she was getting ready for work. She immediately got dad.

Dad looked up veterinarians in the phone book and he found Dr. Colladay in Mountaintop, about ten miles away. He ran a Pet hospital. Mom made the call.

Dad checked out where Pop was working and found a can of turpentine with the paint brushes softening in it. The dog's breath and the smell of his facial fur gave it away. He had clearly snuck into a room and drunk turpentine, which is a poison.

The doctor told mom to bring the dog right up. Before he left both mom and dad smelled more turpentine on the sticky fur by Breezie's mouth. He had definitely drunk turpentine. Would he live? There was a lot left in the can with the paint brushes so that part was good.

Dad and mom took him right up to the hospital and met with Dr. Colladay. The doctor knew the antidote and he did whatever else was in the book for turpentine poisoning.

By this time, it was getting dark and the doctor said he would keep him overnight and see if he could flush out the poison.

My mom and dad went home but before so, they were instructed to call back in the morning to see if Breezie made it through the night. Mom and dad said there was not much sleeping. And there was a lot of praying. He was just a puppy

Pop Katille, when informed, had to be convinced that it was not his fault. Pop had come to love the little guy like we all did. I did not know it then but Breezie would become my dog. When my extra shoulder muscles were sore as they were growing, Breezie would somehow know, and he would help me make them feel better.

Finally mom and dad got the news about the dog. He had made it through the night and. Mom made the call in the AM and Dr. Colladay said he was OK and he would be OK but the doctor asked if my parents would leave Breezie at the hospital for the rest of the day for observation.

Dad and mom picked him up early that evening and his tail was wagging. Breezie had made it. Whew!

Life is good. That night he slept with Mom and dad in their room and the next day, if you'll pardon me, his excretory markings were clearly visible. All systems were working full cycle.

One night in the hospital was not enough to train this little puppy to GO outside.

The Spider Plant and the Wall Incident

Dad tells the next best puppy story. After a few more months it was getting closer to Christmas. Mom and dad loved Christmas. I get it from them. I love Christmas.

Dad was working a little late in the IBM office in Scranton and he called mom at home to make sure everything was OK. It was not OK.

Mom was crying in a big way, and she could hardly speak and she was angry with Breezie so much so that she did not even mention his name. She called him "the dog." Mom said "the dog ate my spider plant and then he pooped on the floor and wiped his butt on the wall." She was very upset.

She added that the dog then kicked up all the dirt onto the floor from the spider plant container and killed the plant. She then said for dad to get home as soon as possible. She said she did not want the dog anymore. The dog had to go or mom said she would be going soon.

Dad was not sure what to do.

Though he had a lot more work to do at the IBM office in Scranton, Dad was smart enough to choose not to spend any more time there that night. He came right home. However, while on his way home, he did stop at Raves, a great garden center right off the Wilkes-Barre exit of Route 81 IBM in Scranton was about 25 miles away from home. Raves was on the way, about a mile from our home in Ashley.

Raves was a full-service gardening center with very nice plants. Dad bought a beautiful new Spider Plant for mom—even better than the one that was formerly in a big pot full of dirt on the living room floor.

Mom was thrilled to get the new spider plant and she had already calmed down and cleaned up the rug from the dog diggings. She was almost OK by the time dad got home.

However, she could not stand the fact that after the puppy had made such a monstrous poop, Breezie topped it off by wiping his butt on the wall right behind the brand new couch. Mom could hardly get the words out when dad came home.

It was all cleaned up but mom left the brown stains on the wall, so Dad could see them. Mom hoped that Dad too would get upset with the "bad" doggie who had actually wiped his butt on the wall. She was still kinda hoping that dad would agree that the dog had to go. Living with the pee and poop had finally gotten to her.

Sure enough, as dad was forced to examine the wall, there were dark brown poop skid-marks right behind the new couch exactly where mom had said. Dad thought that no dog would ever do that on purpose.

Dad looked closer, expecting to generate some olfactory senses. In other words, he started sniffing the wall. I bet it was interesting to see. His nose was not picking up anything. What else could be brown and not look like dirt? It did look just like poop skid marks.

Soon, dad found papers that said Krackel and Mr. Goodbar with the words Dark Chocolate written on them, and he figured out the big mystery.

Breezie had dug up the spider plant for sure. His digging sprayed fresh dirt all over the clean white rug. He weighed so little the dirt was not mushed in the rug.

Mom used the broom and the sweeper and got it all up. Phew!

The mystery dad discovered was that the dog was attracted to the Hershey Miniature dish from the coffee table and he ripped a bunch of them open and devoured them.

Thankfully Breezie did not eat enough to make him sick. As you know, Dogs, should not eat chocolate. Mom and dad were lucky the doggie did not have another turpentine reaction.

In large enough amounts, chocolate and cocoa products can kill your dog. The toxic component of chocolate is theobromine.

Humans easily metabolize theobromine, but dogs process it much more slowly, allowing it to build up to toxic levels in their system. I am so glad Breezie made it twice.

With her new Spider Plant and with the mess cleaned up already, and knowing the wall was now part chocolate, mom was a different person. She was not upset like she was on the phone. She loved the new plant and loved the dog again. I knew that when she told the story and called Breezie over for a big hug.

Dad had showed her the candy paper trail and together, they concluded that the skid marks were chocolate drippings from the puppy's mouth and not poop. Breezie was eating the treats on top of the couch by the white wall with melted chocolate drooling from his mouth.

Mom and dad had a wonderful laugh and went to bed knowing the dog had a treat and mom had a great new plant.

Breezie: the Construction Worker

By Christmas Eve, Breezie was doing much better on the squeaking (very noisy) at night and his droppings were not as regular an occurrence. Mom had decorated the rooms that were finished for Christmas and dad said it was beautiful.

The pictures prove it. It was beautiful for sure. Pop was making great progress in remodeling and he always put the turpentine in a locked closet. When Breezie was permitted to roam again outside of mom & dad's bedroom, Pop learned to push the dog droppings into a pile for dad to pick up each night. Eventually, Breezie began to go outside and Pop would let him out whenever he came over.

After resigning themselves to having two great Christmas turkey dinners, one at the Katille's (mom and dad with Biddie and Pop Katille) and the other at the Trosks (mom and dad with Skippo and Pop Trosk), - they went to bed in their queen-sized bed to get a good night sleep. On this particular night, Breezie was sleeping under the bed or so they thought.

In the middle of the night, they were both awakened by the sound of construction. Hard as it is to believe, it was in the middle of the night.

What could it be?

There was pounding and there was also a gnawing sound. When mom and dad's bed was assembled by Joshy Bohunk, because the house was old, Joshy told mom and dad that he had to find some blocks of wood to even out the four posts of the bed so the bed by itself did not sway back and forth.

By this time late on Christmas Eve, mom and dad were awake. They realized that the construction sound was coming from under the bed. Surly the construction worker had to be wearing a hard hat. It was definitely not Santa.

But, who could it be as nobody but mom and dad and Breezie lived in the house along with a few small mice. Whoops I was not supposed to mention that we had some mice. Breezie was not a cat so it did not bother him. Though prevalent in the homes in the Cummings Street neighborhood, even the Zabolas, the mice were never known before to make such a racket.

Mom and dad looked at each other and they smiled. They realized it was the puppy teething. He was gnawing on the blocks of wood as puppies do but he was not squeaking and squealing as he was months earlier. The puppy was happy. They were gnaws of happiness.

FYI, a puppy's baby teeth start coming in between 3 to 5 weeks of age, and all their baby teeth are full grown by the time they're 8 weeks old. Breezie had all his baby teeth when he was under the bed.

At about ages 4 to 6 months, the process starts all over again, with a dog's adult teeth coming in. A puppy grows a total of 28 baby teeth—12 incisors, 4 canines and 12 premolars. In comparison to us humans, a puppy doesn't have his baby teeth for very long.

In just a month after he finishes growing them, a puppy starts losing his baby teeth. Eventually a dog has 42 teeth so the little furballs are growing teeth from about 3 weeks to about 26 weeks. That means that Breezie was working on his teeth under our bed on Christmas Eve. See the picture on the left of Breezie when he as five years old. Dad was holding him in this picture.

Eventually mom and dad caught on to the rhythm and woke up on Christmas morning with their new little man, Breezie, sound asleep under the bed. Mom and dad envisioned the little guy under the bed with a little hard hat on to make sure he got all his work done. They could not help laughing.

Breezie was as cute a dog as anybody could have ever met in life. The next morning my parents spotted some obvious bite marks in the blocks of wood.

Close by was a little wet spot and a few small logs so mom and dad had more proof that the little man's internal system was functioning well. The new Katille family had survived the construction activity

Chapter 4 The Puppy's Christmas & the March 1980 "Move"

Our two turkey dinners for the day—one at Pop Katille's and Pop Trosk's on Christmas day were as picturesque as the picture above. Thanks Pop and Nana. Thanks Pop and Nana.

Pop Katille told mom and dad on Christmas day that he was doing so well on the construction of the 54 Cummings street place—papering and painting work that he believed that by the end of January, he would be done, and they could move all their furniture under sheets and blankets in other rooms into the remodeled areas of the home. Much of the stuff was stored down the street at Pop and Mom Katille's place and some on

Hillside street at Pop Smokey Trosk's and Nana Skippo Trosk's.

Christmas dinner was great at Pop Katille's at noon (not a second later) and it was also great at Pop Trosks at 6:00 PM. Both the Trosks and the Katilles loved Breezie. And, he was there at both stops that day to enjoy some turkey. Boy, did he ever.

My dad was taught by his brother Joseph Aloysius to bark. So, on the walking trip down to Pop Katilles's Dad started doing his bark so he says. I was not there. Mom sad before they got there every dog in the neighborhood was barking and dad did not know what they were saying. I heard his bark and it is very good.

The night before Christmas—about 5:00 PM after mass on Christmas Eve, Pop and Grandma Biddie Katille made a little fest for all his kids—Dad, his brothers, sisters, and their kids.

Pop Katille bought a bunch of candles at Big Bob's Liquidating, which was on Blackman Street at the time; and it was the perfect night. It was beautiful. Dad's brothers and sisters and Dad and mom left about 7:30 for their next stops. My mom and dad's next stop every year was Pop and Nana Trosk's on Hillside Street.

Our house before the remodeling is shown below. Pop and Nana Trosk lived just about a mile away next to Mary and Cathy's place in the Heights. Pop and Biddie Katille lived on the other side of Cummings street just about seven doors down.

Pop Trosk loved Breezie as much but in a more mushy way than Pop Katille. Breezie spent every day when mom and dad had gone to work for years at Pop Katille house right down the street. Dad dropped him off every day when he had a coffee with Pop as he was on his way to work.

Both pops loved the doggie to pieces. Pop Trosk every year bought Breezie three squeak toys. He placed them carefully and easily dog-spottable with all the gifts under the Trosk tree.

He also put up a little platform with HO gauge track and a little train and he ran it for everybody before they had the gift opening. Here is his train and tree.

Each year, Pop Trosk offered everybody a little schnorkie right before he sang Silent Night. He did it well. His eyes always filled up wet near the end of his singing.

By the time he finished singing Silent Night, all of his adult children including mom and even my dad were crying. Dad admits to wetting up a bit on Christmas Eve at the Trosks though he tried to hide it.

This particular year, Pop Trosk had a new friend, our new puppy, Breezie, our dog, who after Silent Night, seemed to know it was going to be a great night for him. It was.

Mom's brothers and sisters had just met Breezie and he was still a frisky little dog and they had yet to bond with the little guy.

They were more than a bit taken back when Pop Trosk called Breezie first instead of my uncle and aunts to go find his gifts. Pop had wrapped Breezie's gifts with the same paper as everybody else's It was not the way it had ever been for the Trosk siblings before Breezie.

Without looking at the name tags, because the paper was the same, nobody seemed to trust that Breezie would find only his presents. They knew Breezie could not read the name tags so they feared he might not avoid their gifts in his frantic hunt.

Breezie did not miss one of the three items that Pop had carefully wrapped and placed around the tree. He found them all. He touched nobody else's gifts. Mom's brothers and sisters were sure he would grab one of their gifts by mistake, but he did not. Everybody was amazed at that.

He plowed through—over and around all the other stacked gifts stepping on them lightly as he went about in his search; but he did not break anything. One by one he brought each of his own little gifts into a small clearing on the floor where nobody was sitting and there had been no other gifts.

With a clever combination of his teeth and his paws, he unwrapped each gift, one by one. Each was a different shaped squeak toy. He made no mistakes. The siblings and mom and dad were in awe.

Breezie eventually won all the Trosks siblings over From then on, they trusted him and they learned to love him but nobody loved him as much as Pop Trosk except maybe Grandma Biddie, Grandma Skippo and Grandpop Eddie Katille.

Once he was able to squeak the toy and prove he was king of that particular squeak toy, Breezie went back again for the next package and the next, repeating his unwrapping ritual each time. He seemed to know there were only three for him and he calmed down when he had them all.

By the third unwrapping of the third squeak toy, the Trosk siblings had confidence that Breezie would pick only his own gifts and they too were able to enjoy his antics as much as mom and dad and Pot Trosk and Nana Trosk. It was a magical night.

When Pop ran the HO train, it made it even more magical.

Mom and dad have often talked about how wonderful Christmas Eve was up at the Trosk homestead with kielbasa, smoked and fresh, and Eggnog and the schnorkies and other great cheer. What a gift if today we could go back and relive something like that.

Moving in the furniture

In March, 1976, mom and dad and Breezie moved from the covered construction areas which were now finished to wherever mom and dad wanted in each of the five rooms on Cummings Street.

I don't know where it all was but I know from what they told me that there was a new TV that Pop and Nana bought for the wedding a ton of new furniture for the house Mom had picked. Plus, anticipating that I would have a brother and hopefully a sister, mom had bought a canopy bed that was all white. Additionally from what they remember, there was a lot of their stuff stored at Pop Katille's down the street.

It all had to go to places in the house that mom had determined. After living with minimal furniture while the rooms were being fixed up, they were thrilled to now have their home arranged with all their new digs on 54 Cummings Street. Four or five months of construction activity was enough It was all done. Pop Katille had done a great job. He knew it and enjoyed a few brewskys with dad.

Dad had some great friends back then and he still does have great friends but some of these past greats have passed away. There was Denny Bucko Grimes, Joshy and Georgie Bohunk, Geraldo Tobe, Frannsys Xavier Kurilla, Mikey Kurilla, and others. Uncle Joe and Uncle Ed were always willing to help dad and he helped them when needed. They got everything moved in and a lot of other relatives including the Flanders boys showed up too. Beer was like a magnet and Chile kept them there while they worked. Mom said that we had both. If it were not such a big move, it could have just been a great party.

Yes, The great crew of nephews and nieces in the Katille family all showed up for the final placement of all the furniture and a celebration of what mom and dad considered their move-in day. It was all done by the end of the day on the second Saturday in March.

Besides the humans, there was other help. For example, there was a quarter of Erlanger Beer, dad's favorite at the time, and a pot of Mom's great Chile Con Carne. The crew could not wait to gobble it all up and they did. Both the chile and the beer kicked before the last helper left the premises. There were also Abe's hot dogs and they were all gone at days' end too!

Though everybody was tired, there was some other beer left over from someplace. Dad is not sure when the keg kicked or if what he found was cans or bottles or both. He said that we as a family were not completely on E (empty).

Relaxing after the move, mom and had dad sat down at the new kitchen table—a special table made by hand by Uncle Bucko. For five months it was well covered with table cloths and protection but on this day, Mom took all the covers off and showed everybody what Uncle Bucko had made – a magnificent trestle table.

She could not wait to get the 20 year old used rug from underneath the beautiful trestle table that Bucko would afterwards paint dark oak.

Picture us all sitting at this table. Mom decided she needed some chocolate. Everybody was happy because everything was where it should be—even the new refrigerator brought in by my buddy Franny.

Mom had a frozen rabbit that she had recently moved to this new refrigerator. Like I said, the guy who had originally carried that refrigerator and freezer up the front steps and into the house, Big Frannie, was sitting right in front of the new Fridge.

While enjoying one of the last beers in the whole house, Francis J. Kurilla was accosted by a chocolate rabbit as Mom was fetching it from the freezer.

You see, as mom tried to grab the rabbit, it was a bit icy and it slipped out of her hands and smashed big Franny Kurilla, a gentle giant, in the nose and lip. Some of dad's friends were saying he had carried in the refrigerator with one hand and he gets wounded by accident.

Most of dad's buddies had seen Franny, a wonderful man, rip huge doors off big buildings for less provocation than a cut lip and bruised nose. .

There was silence until the Big guy realized he had not died and nobly had tried to harm him. When the nose-bleeding Franny Kurilla laughed and laughed and laughed, there were no more concerns, Then, he too enjoyed the chocolate and beer along with his beautiful wife Joanne, who he loved profusely.

He and she laughed harder than anybody according to dad. What a great day they all had. What a great hand they had lent to mom and dad to accomplish the move. Life was just beginning for mom and dad Katille. Frannie and Joanne would be a big part of their lives. Thank you dear Lord.

Chapter 5 Life on 54 Cummings Street

So, mom and dad were now in the big house. Pop Katille had it all polished up.

In the stories my parents told, I learned that mom and dad felt that it did not take them long to adjust to the light green house with two bedrooms at 54 Cummings Street. .

While they were getting accustomed to their new life on Cummings Street, Pop Katille built one more thing for them.

He and dad had some bits and pieces of some porch-wood that Pop had stored at his place. As you look at the house on the prior page, you can see the big picture window. Behind the window, there was a big dining room/ family room right by the open stairway to the upstairs, which was in the back of the room. Pop Katille built a compact bar in that room on the right side of the window.

It was right there to see when you walked in the front door on the right side of the porch. Sometimes they called it the gold room. Dad and Pop Katille later moved the bar o something that we later called "The Sun Room."

My dad loved buying carpet remnants from Giant Floor. He picked up a wonderful green rug for that room and to please mom, he papered one of the walls tropical. It was very pretty and until we left Cummings Street years later, everything was still looking good on that wall.

Thirteen years later when the family moved to South Wilkes-Barre, that carpeting and the wall paper still looked like new. The family room was where we spent most of our time on Cummings Street until the Sun room was built, so that says a lot.

Dad tells me that about ten years after that, when mom and dad finally sold our Cummings Street home, that the twenty-three-year-old carpeting in that room still looked the same and it still looked sharp. Nice job Dad!

BTW, other than the wallpaper, Pop Katille painted all the walls gold in that room except the wall with the wallpaper. I had forgotten about that.

The built-in bar that Pop Katille built from scratch out of porch-wood, was always the center of attention.

Dad had bought paneling before mom found the tropical wall-paper. So, dad gave Pop Katille the paneling. It looked like brick. During the construction of the brick paneling in Pop's middle room, dad tells a great story about Pop Katille, my grandpop. Dad had given Pop four brand new home remodeling books (a great set that was not cheap) for his retirement. Pop received them graciously but never seemed to be reading them.

When Pop Katille was doing the brick-like paneling in his house, however, he cheered up his middle child, my dad. He told dad that he made good use of the books.

He said that the 8-foot paneling was about one inch short of where he wanted it to lay and the four one-inch thick books helped him boost the paneling up to the level he needed to have it for easy nailing. Pop Katlle had used these expensive books to hold up the panels— not to find out how to put them in right. Humph! We laughed,

Dad got a kick out of it, but my guess is that secretly Dad had hoped Pop would have found some secret techniques for construction rather than having used the books to prop up the paneling. Just saying!

Coming in the front door of the new living quarters, you would walk to the right to get to the new bar Pop had built. On the other side, was the open stairway which led to the second of two floors. Here is a picture of dad showing off at Christmas time on the beautiful open stairway. As a 39-year old today, I can say Dad liked to act like a hot-dog. We loved him for it.

From where my dad is on the open stairway, he could look to his left to see wall with the tropical wall paper. The green rug I mentioned earlier had a nice tropical look to it and with the wall paper, it dad a definite tropical look.

On this page, you can see the dining room wallpaper with Christmas stockings and gifts galore.

The other walls in the room were painted gold. After pop painted the other walls, dad did the papering such as the tropical look in this dining room. The bar was to the far right in this picture—a big room for sure.

Before you would get into the kitchen, there was a very short hallway and on the right was the cellar door.

The cellar steps were small and it was tough to get up and down. Continuing through to the kitchen, right after the kitchen table was the back door that opened to a porch which we eventually converted to a deck. The back door was on the left side of the kitchen.

If we chose not to go right to the sink, as noted, straight through the kitchen was the back door. For most of the time that we lived there, it opened to the outside onto a covered deck, the pool deck, and the back yard.

We made a lot of use of that back deck and dad eventually connected the porch deck to the swimming pool deck, which you can see in the next picture.

Mortrock and I in 1982, are shown on the pool deck that was connected to the porch deck. I'll tell you about all that soon.

If you could see to the right, it was the spot where this lower deck met the pool seats and where those who wanted to swim simply jumped in. I could not find pictures of the pool but this gives the idea. Right after the picture of Mortrock and I is a Muskin pool like ours.

Picture Mortrock and I on the inside of the wooden deck on the left below:

OK folks, it is time to get out of the pool.

Before Christmas after the first anniversary on Cummings Street, Dad had begun to make some holiday purchases.

He first bought a 5X9 platform with 18 inch legs. He said it was like the platform he had on High Street where he lived as a kid. I was not born yet, but I loved dad telling this story.

Dad put the platform up well before Christmas and then with his checkbook in his hand, with mom by his side, Dad went to Frank's Roundhouse about a month before Christmas, 1975, and he bought a big LGB train.

It was a starter train without a caboose. It looked like an overstuffed HO Train but it was twice the size of a Lionel. Everything looked big. Dad then spend almost a hundred bucks before I was born to buy an LGB caboose.

There were only two tracks like HO but they were about twice a wide as the three-track Lionel's. The picture on the next page is how it looked on the shelf at Frank's Roundhouse.

Frank Rash owned the Roundhouse place on the Sans Souci Highway. He had been dad's high school baseball coach. So, we got a good deal on an LGB train.

Later, six years or so, after I was born, I played T-Ball for Mr. Rash's team at St. Theresa's Little League. As you might expect, our team's name was Frank's RoundHouse. Frank Rash had sponsored the team.

As we discussed in the last chapter, Pop Trosk always put up a nice HO train at his house during the holidays and I always liked that as a kid. Dad's train was huge compared to that.

Dad said he put the two 4'X5' platforms together and bolted the eight 18" legs onto the corners. The combined platform size was 8' X 5".

Dad had figured that the big curve on the LGB needed five feet so a 4X8 foot standard platform would not do. And so from left to right there was curved track then straight track which met a matching curved set of tracks from the other side, coming together in an oval. It was another part of the magical about living on Perfect Street. When I was born four years later, dad was still creating the platform every year and it was a thing of beauty just like it was the first year. I saw the pictures.

Dad always put this green paper on the platform before he put the track down. It was coated with a picky grass like substance and when the platform was in full bloom, it looked like a field of green grass. Mom always added a few pretty houses and stuff like that.

I saw it on the pictures that mom and dad kept from their first Christmas on 54 Cummings St. The tree was placed on the left side on one of the 4X5 bolted pieces and on the other side was the yard which was sometimes green and sometimes snowy. It changed from year to year.

Dad said that shortly after he and mom moved to the house with the furniture, he and Uncle Joe and Uncle Ed began to play darts with Pop Katille at the Wilkes-Barre Republic Club.

Dad's mom, whom we all called Grandma Biddie because Pop Katille called her Biddie, would walk to our house to spend time with Pat (Mom) and Breezie when dad and Pop Katille went to play darts. Mom loved that and so did dad. Breezie loved Grandmom Katille as much as he loved Pop Trosk. Pop Katille loved the puppy also but would not as readily admit it.

They told me a lot of stories about the early days before I was born. I loved listening to them.

Chapter 6 The Stork Brings Me to Cummings Street

It was about five and a half years after Mom and Dad were married that God gave the Stork specific instructions as to where to deliver me. It was May 28, 1980 but I remember nothing about it.

He delivered me to Mercy Hospital in Wilkes-Barre to a guy named Dr. Horan; but shortly afterwards, mom and dad took me to our Cummings Street home.

The full story that I was told was that Mom had a long labor of almost 24 hours and the Stork finally brought me through the window of my mom's hospital room in the early evening on May 28. Dad and mom were thrilled, as they have told me many times.

They did not forget to tell me that there were stork feathers on the hospital floor.

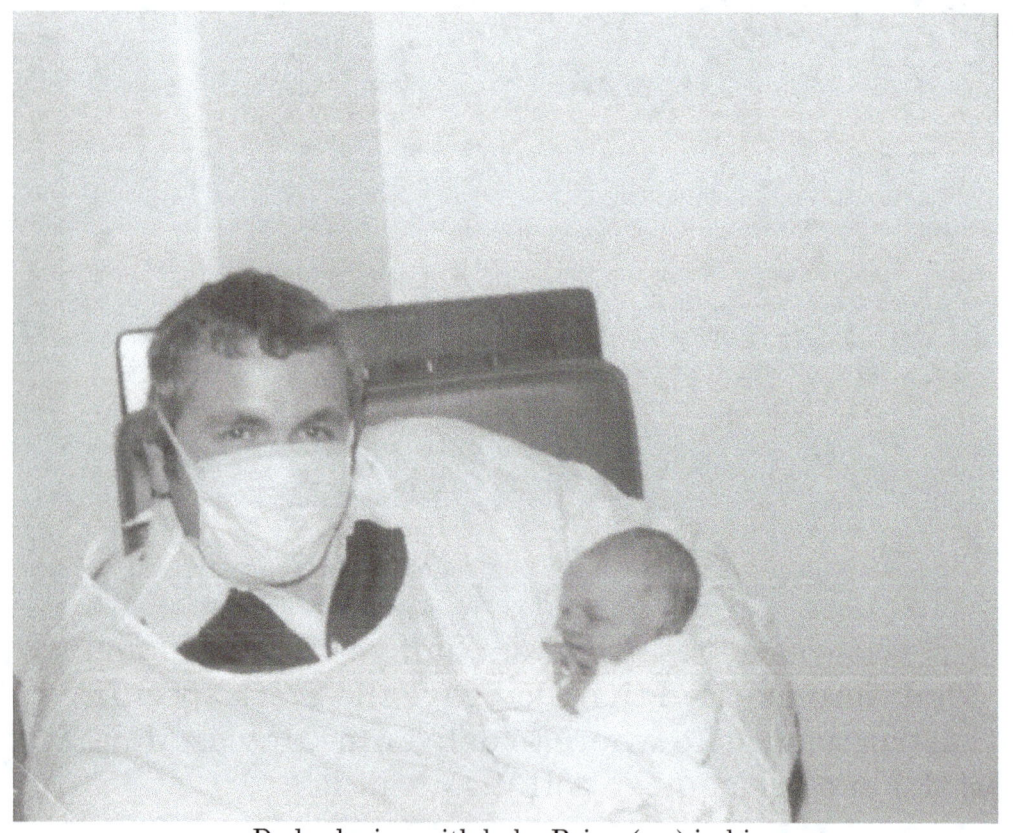
Dad relaxing with baby Brian (me) in his arms

Everything went well with me, thankfully. Dr. Horan literally showed dad he had a little boy and he had dad do his duty with something called the umbilical cord. Dr. John Rogers, who dad played baseball with dad at King's College did the in-hospital operation, so I could go home.

Dad says Dr. Rogers was a great short-stop on the King's College Baseball Team. After a few days, it was time to head for Cummings Street. By the way, at the time of my birth, my back shoulder area was the same size as all other little boys and girls. Nobody suspected that wings were in my future. At this time, neither did I.

All the while at the hospital, the two pops and the two nanas were visiting and there were nurses taking care of me when mom was sleeping (not much sleep she says.) I was never alone it seemed. Dad and mom always had lots of help they say, in the hospital.

Dad pulled the car up to the hospital door. Mom was already there with me all bundled up. They brought us down in a wheel chair for safety. It was late morning and not very hot yet for May 28. Dad already had a baby car seat in the back and that is where they put me right next to mom. But first, they took a picture of mom holding me in the front seat before we took off on our way home:

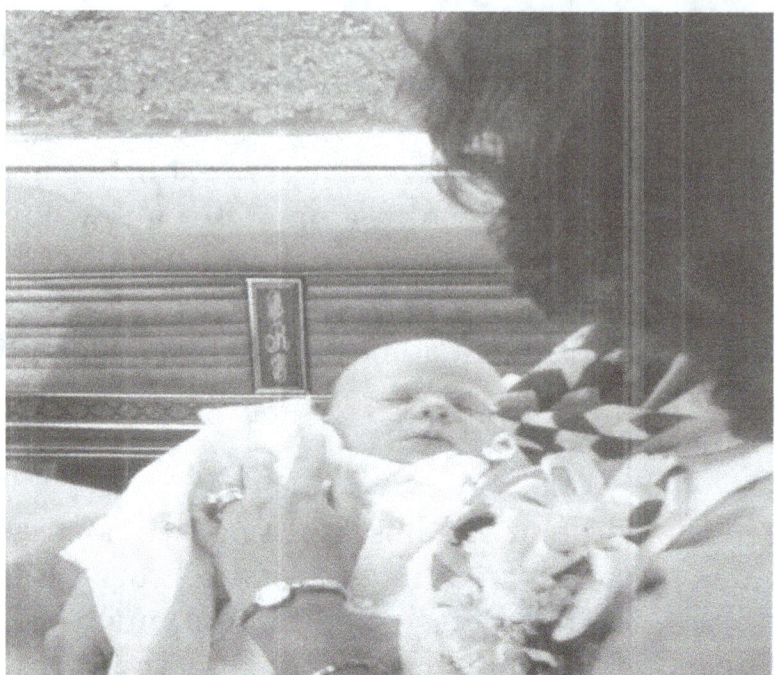
Mom and Baby Brian in the car for this picture

The parking spot in front of the house on Cummings Street was open so dad parked right there. Our door was on the sidewalk side but at the time, there was no sidewalk.

Mom and Brian on Cummings Street

Dad came around and opened the door and mom got me out of the seat constraints. She carried me up the eight steps to the front door on 54 Cummings Street. Dad trailed behind in case if anything went wrong, he could catch us. Dad then passed us and opened the front door.

As we went in dad said he felt alone and somewhat scared as he and mom were bringing a real live child into the house for the first time. Mom and dad looked at each other and their looks said, "now what?"

There were no pops or nanas there to make it all OK for my parents this time. They said they immediately felt the weight of responsibility to make sure little Brian, the first born, was OK.

By the end of the day, the pops and the nanas and a number of relatives and friends had stopped in to see the new baby. It was me.

My white crib, which we got from Mr. Plescik, Big Franny's wife's dad, was all set up in the "baby room upstairs. Before long, mom said, I was in my crib and sound asleep giving the new parents a short break from my whining.

Because as they told me, I had my nights and day's mixed up, it would be a long time before mom and dad got any real rest again.

I took a lot of mom and dad's time in the early days. As I said, I had my nights and days mixed up. I apparently did not like it at all when mom and dad were asleep.

Below is a picture of me and mom and dad and our wonderful dog Breezie right after we got home.

This picture was taken in our huge dining / family room on Cummings Street. You cannot see the green rug. Notice the tropical wallpaper that mom had selected for this wall.

Pop Trosk, who was grandpop Trosk, but who I eventually called Pop Trosk, never liked to use his real first name. He preferred the name *Smoke or Smokey* instead of Stanley. All the kids called him Grand Pop or simply Pop Trosk.

I often wondered whether he smoked a lot or he like smoked kielbasa, which he always served on the major holidays. Regardless, *the Smoke* liked me and I knew it. I loved him to pieces.

The next big event that started on Cummings Street was my Christening. Below are a bunch of pictures from that great day. The priest who baptized me was Father John Terry. He also baptized my brother Mortrock and sister Katers.

His father, Mr. Buddy Terry worked with my father at IBM in Scranton. He is a wonderful priest. Here is a picture of me and mom getting ready for my baptism.

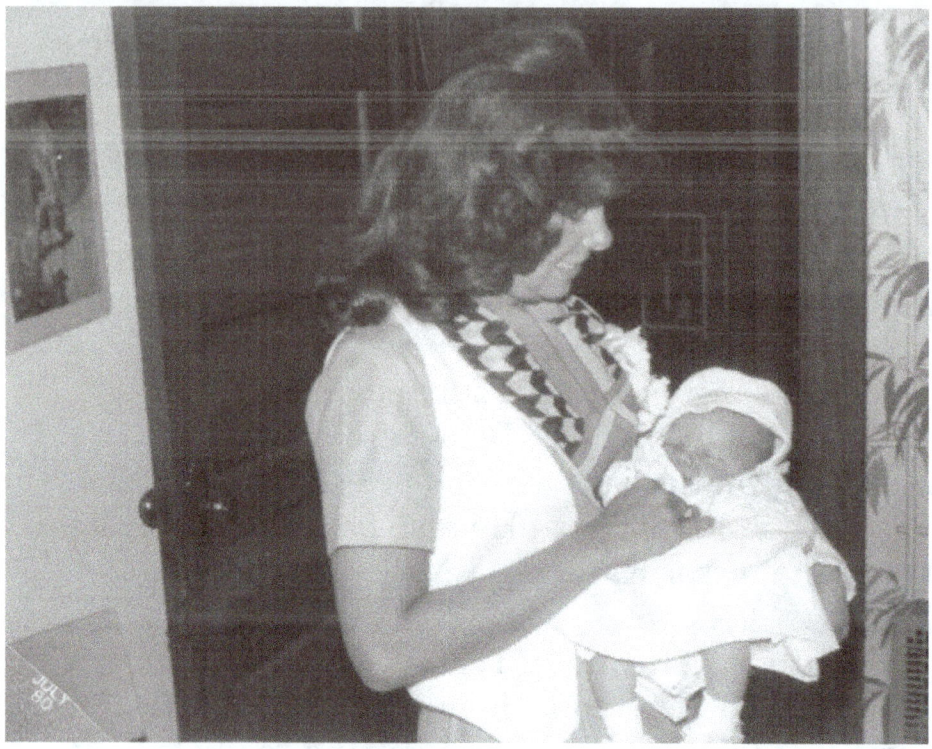

On the next page is a nice picture of me and mom and Nana Trosk who was helping mom get me ready for the Christening:

Below is Father John Terry at the Christening
with my Godmother Aunt Sue and Aunt Cathy and Dad.

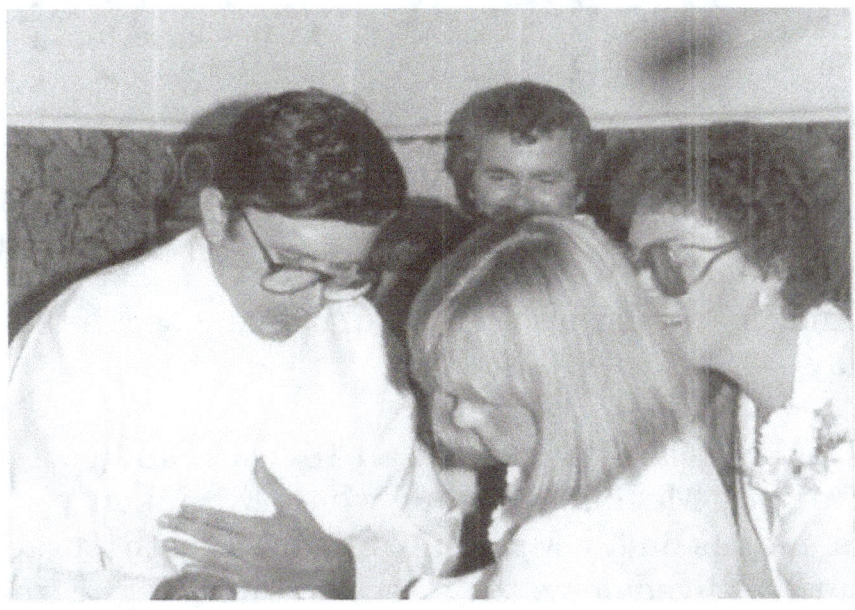

g

When the Christening was over, we all went back to Cummings Street for the party. Here is a picture of me with my Godmother Aunt Sue and Godfather, Uncle Joe and a bunch of my uncles and aunts at the front of St. Patrick's Church as we were leaving the Christening. See Aunt Hey Hey and her mom Carrie in the front:

And, that was that. The regular living began the next day.

In April 1980, dad bought an 18-foot round pool right from the Muskin Company where Mr. Mike Kurilla and his buddy Mr. Romy Shedleski both worked. The Kurilla's lived down the street on Cummings Street. The Evans,' Karen and Ken, lived upstairs in the same house with the Kurilla's. Mr. Kurilla and Mr. Shedleski got dad a great deal on the pool.

Better than that, they both knew how to install Muskin above-ground pools and they had our pool up and running in about a week. Everybody helped to install the pool.

By the time I got home in May, the pool was up and running and my cousins, the Dales and the Flanders had already had a few swims in the new pool.

Being only a week or so old, I was unaware that year that we had a pool, but I have been told that I was always around all the pool action. I first spotted the new Muskin Pool after Dad opened it in late May 1980, I was in wonderment. Dad had it ready to go earlier but the water was too cold for anybody.

Memorial Day was the first warm day. It was on May 26, two days before I was born. The Dales and the Flanders' (my Aunt Nancy's crew) had already tried out the new pool. Dad told me the pool water was quite cold before the holiday, but by Memorial day, it was warm enough to swim.

There were always squirrels by the big trees in our back yard. Sometimes they would be on the seats on the top of the pool until dad would chase them. Before long all the kids were singing a song dad had made up.

They would sing it when they would make a whirl pool to help clean up any debris that was in the pool.

After the whirl pool, the leaves, etc., would all be in a little pile in the middle of the pool. Dad would get the kids singing:

This is not a squirrel pool
This is a whirl-pool.

Go ahead sing it and repeat it until enough is enough. It was so much fun, my brother and sister and everybody else sang it for years.

Before the summer was over, two of the four Zabola kids, besides Mary and Dwan—David and Kim, from next door would come to swim as did the Callahans, who lived further down Cummings Street.

Mr. Zabola and Mrs. Zabola came too and they would swim to cool off. Here is a picture of Nana Trosk on the back deck with me in July 1980:

Dad told me that all summer long when mom was outside with everybody and dad was at work at IBM, she kept me mostly in my "baby seat" next door in the porch closet (which became the door to the "Sun Room." And the door was always open to give me a breeze. The door was just to the left of the picture above with Nana Trosk.

When you would go into the back entrance of 54 Cummings Street, the closet which became the entrance to the Sun Room built by the uncles and dad, at first looked like a miniature foyer. That's where mom kept me most of the time, out of the sun and safe from the porch and pool traffic It was my shade nook. Life changes everything and sometimes for the good.

Thanksgiving & The 1980 Christmas Season

In 1980 when I was a baby, Mom said that it was great having company all summer, but it was an awful lot of work. By the time Thanksgiving came, I had taken so many pictures with my eyes that I was starting to make sense out of some things in life, or so I thought. I was about six months old at Thanksgiving.

I was crawling wherever I needed to go. Mom and dad put a big gate at the top of the stair steps so I would not fall down the steps. They also put cushions on all the sharp table corners to protect my eyes when I was in my walker. There were even covers on the electrical outlets.

From right before Thanksgiving, mom was decorating the house for Christmas. Dad often joked that if he stood still during this time for any length of time, he ran the risk of mom putting an ornament on him.

As a Senior Systems Engineer for IBM , dad had an IBM system account in Millville, PA called Girton Manufacturing. He invited our great friends the Komorek's, Al and Karen to go to Millville with him and mom to get a nice fresh-cut tree. They agreed. Dad is Michael Komorek's God-Father.

Nana and Pop Trosk watched me while my parents went for the fresh cut tree.

Mom and dad always talked about what great trips they were. After picking the pre-cut tree in the

Guzmar's front yard in Millville, PA, they would put the tree inside my dad's VW Bus and head off to the Hotel MaGee in Bloomsburg.

It was dinner at Dick Benefield's Groaning Board. They bragged about the super smorgasbord that accompanied the great dinner. One year, Al Harding the Controller from Girton Manufacturing and his lovely wife, connected to join mom and dad for the tree and a great dinner.

When dad and mom got home, dad put the tree in the house and the very next day, he set up the platform with the green paper already on it from years before. Putting up the tree was never a secret in our home.

The first year that he had put up the platform and train, dad had laid the track down and made sure the split for the two platforms was right where the back and front tracks separated.

He had tacked it down so the it would stay in place even after the two sides were separated. That way, he had a lot of work already done for the following years like this one. So, this time, when he set up the platform, he simply joined the tracks from the two 4X5 pieces and created the big 5X8 platform. He then put the eight legs back on

Mom had me in my baby seat as Dad put the engine on the track and connected the lock-on to the transformer. He made sure that the train would travel smoothly across all the tracks—curved and straight.

It was great. I can almost remember seeing it all happen as mom watched me while dad ran the train engine for the first time to make sure it was OK. It was fine.

Dad then then put the tree in the fresh tree holder and moved the tree and holder onto the left side of the platform. The train would go around the tree. To make sure the tree would not fall, dad put two nails in the wall and he wrapped wires around the tree and then wrapped the wires around the nails. The way dad set it up, the tree was not going anywhere.

Mom always offered dad advice about how to do everything. When setting up, dad tried to put another car on the train. Mom stopped him and said not to do that until all the lights and ornaments were on the tree as she would have to walk on the platform to get that job done.

Dad weighed over 200 pounds then. Today he is over 300 pounds but to me, he still looks good. He actually looks like Santa Claus and his big belly makes it even more so.

He found the beams where the wood was in the platform and with mom on the floor, dad started at the top of the tree and he put all the lights on the tree.

They all worked, which was unusual. Then dad got the white garland and put it around the tree. He bought a pack of icicles but mom did not want them on with the garland, so dad said OK.

Mom then got out the old ornaments from their time when my parents had no children and she added new ones she had recently bought. She carefully put them all on the tree and she saved the newest ornament, "Baby's First Christmas" as the last ornament. That was because of me.

When she had the tree decorated and it was all beautiful and sparkly, she called dad over and gave him a kiss. They shared some wine together before mom announced that it was time to put the top on the tree. That was a big deal.

I don't know what the top looked like as mom would often get a new top each Christmas. I know it had electric wires, so dad had to get back up on the platform and find where he could plug it in.

When he got it plugged in and it was all lit, he reached up very carefully and set it on the very top of the tree. Mom guided him to get it straight and he did a great job according to mom. The tree itself was done. Now, for the platform scenes.

Dad bought some mountain paper this year and he put a couple boxes together on the left side mostly at the end of the platform and mostly behind the tree.

He cut holes in the boxes so that they would form the basis for the openings in the tunnel he was building. I have pictures of this, but I can't find any with the mountains that he built that year.

Dad put the boxes where he wanted them and then he ran the engine again to make sure that it would fit going inside the mountain and then out of the tunnel. It all worked. Rather than remove the boxes, dad tacked them down and put on the mountain paper carefully.

Here is a picture of a pre-made LGB tunnel. The one dad made was much more realistic:

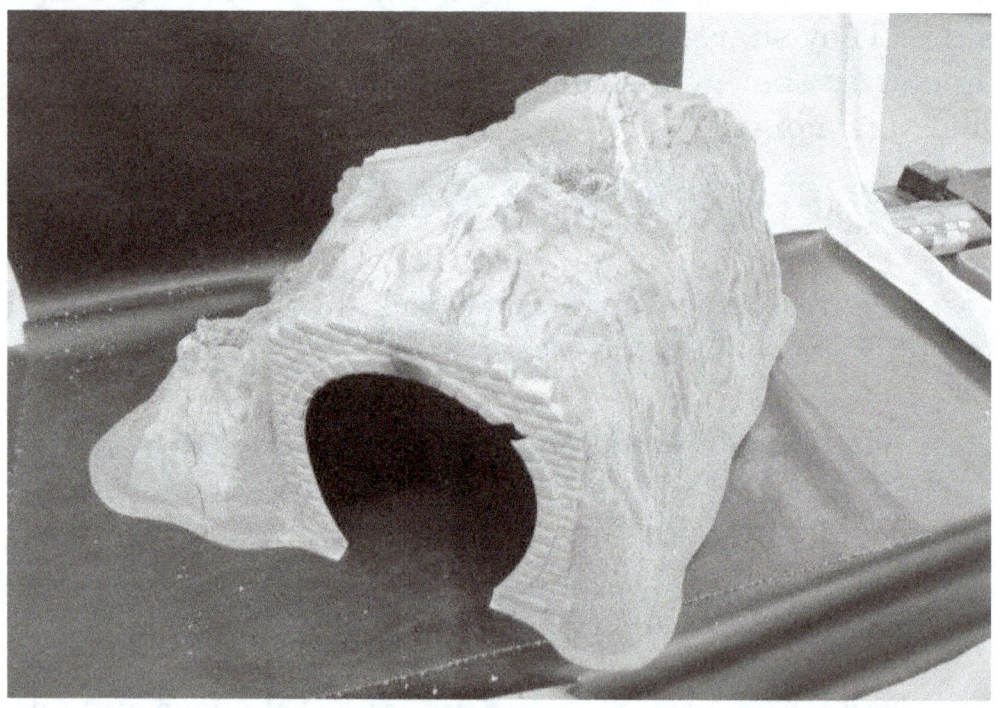

Dad used some Scotch Tape and some tacks to make sure the pieces of mountain paper after being wrinkled to give it the mountain look would continue to stay in place. It took about a half hour as they told me because it was a delicate job. That big tunnel was wonderful.

I may not have seen it well when I was six months old but every year after, dad would do the same thing. Then, one year from being stored in the cellar, the tunnel mostly fell apart and the tree did the job of the tunnel from then on.

Mary Zabola, (AKA Dinder), Katers, Me (Brian P. , and Mortrock A

As you can see on the prior page, as dad liked to say when he looked at this picture: "We used four wonderful gifts from God pretending they were platform decorations. From left to right is my best buddy Mary Zabola, who we also called Dawn, Katers, Me, and then Morty Mortrock.

You can see all this in this picture from Christmas in 1987. It was after we had moved to our new house on Mergy Avenue in South Wilkes-Barre after my special gift was complete . Dad used the same tree and train platform but put the tree on the right side. Even I know that dad could not run the train while we were up there pretending to be train platform kids, but it is a great picture.

As the years went by, my brother Mortrock and my sister Katers and I loved the train platform and the train. I called it the Toot Toot, and Mortrock and Katers called it the Choo-Choo Woo-Woo!

Back in December1980, when dad was done building the mountain and the tunnel for the train platform, he turned all the future proceedings over to mom. She had the decorator touch.

She was waiting to begin the delicate work of setting up houses, the ice-skating rink, the roads, the people including the carolers, and the streetlights and anything else mom thought was needed. Mom was great and I thank God every day that she is great.

Tree on left side in our Cummings St. Home – can't see the tunnel from this angle

Mom put snow from a box on the entire left side of the platform. She covered the sides of the ice-skating rink with snow too and added the ice-skaters. She put Santa's workshop there and a ginger-bread house. You can see them in the picture above if you have good eyes.

They were close right up next to the tree holder, which had its own snow covering via a white tree blanket. It was beautiful. You could hardly tell that the green paper was underneath it all—until you looked to the right side of the platform.

Here is where mom's artistic talents came in. She and dad had bought about ten houses and a church and a railway station. Mom used old coffee grounds and instinctively created roads.

She put the church in the middle of the village and put the train station in the front. This was all on the right side. She put the houses right by the roads, so they looked perfect. She then added some people walking and some cars on the roads and some street lamps.

In this first year of my life, the street lamps did not light nor did the houses but as time went by in the following years, mom figured out how to light up the houses and the street lights. It was spectacular.

When the platform homes etc. were all in place, mom asked dad to put the whole train on the tracks. We had an engine, a tender (where they kept the coal), a cattle car, and a flat bed. After this was the caboose.

Dad got it all together and then said that it was time for her first spin. The engine had a light and it worked as did all the other lights. The train zoomed around the platform and then hit the mountain and the tunnel, it all disappeared for an instant.

We saw the light on the other side of the tunnel and soon the train and all the cars were out of the tunnel heading for another run around the platform. It was great. Mom and dad were thrilled and they said that when I looked at it all, I had a little twinkle in my eye.

They told me that then, there were just two more things to do.

Dad bought a skirt for the platform that was made of cardboard. It was a red-brick-looking skirt that covered up the under side of the 18" high platform. When dad got that finished with thumbtacks to hold it on, there was just one more thing to do.

Just that day, dad came home with a nice white wooden fence that was about five inches high. He put the fence up on every area of the outside top of the platform wherever there was no back wall.

Dad set the fireplace paper so there was a little slit where the wires from the train transformer went up to the track. You could not see the wires or the transformer until dad chose to bring the transformer out from under the platform. It was clever. Wow! What a beautiful job dad! Thanks!.

Mom said after all that work setting up the tree and platform in 1980, we were ready for Christmas. She said the beautiful fresh tree from Millville was perfectly shaped and it smelled great. Though I am not really sure that I remember, when I look at the picture, I can smell the tree. And I love the smell. Wasn't it perfect looking?

On Christmas day, I can sort of recall a pile of wrapped items sitting right next to that fireplace paper with the platform and tree in the background. There was a tree, and when I opened up my presents that year, there were toys, and of course on Christmas Eve and Christmas day, there was the big Toot-Toot buzzing around the platform. It was peeking in and out of the mountain and around the big tree.

You bet it was magical. Mom and dad loved their first Christmas with their first little man. That little man was me.

Chapter 7 Baby Brian's First Christmas--1980

We had the tree up weeks before Christmas eve. On Christmas Eve, mom and dad drove me to St. Patrick's Church about a mile away for 4:30 Mass. Dad and the two Pops, Uncle Joe, and Uncle Ed had been at the Republic Club before that for their afternoon free-open house. Right after church we drove to meet my Katille cousins for Christmas at the Pop Katille house.

I was in the back seat in the baby-seat because we first went to church and right after the Katille celebration, we were heading up to Pop & Nana Trosks.

In the picture above, Pop Katille was taking a short breather on Christmas Eve. That's a Stegmaer in the foreground.

I don't remember much but Pop Katille had a nice house and a nice tree, and it smelled good in the house. It was crowded with lots of kids and my uncles and aunts.

Everybody had already eaten by the time we got there as St. Pat's Mass was always a little late. Aunt Nancy Flanders' children always got at the turkey first but this year, it did not matter as Mom was still feeding me.

Before anybody opened any presents, Grandma Biddie came into the living room and faced the tree. Pop Katille announced that she was going to finish decorating Pop's tree.

Grandma Biddie (her real name is Irene) had something white and shiny behind her back and when she got to the tree, like a baseball player, she wound up and threw it on the tree. It was angel hair and it landed about a foot from the top of the tree. It was beautiful and sparkling right where it was so nobody moved it. Here is what it looked like:

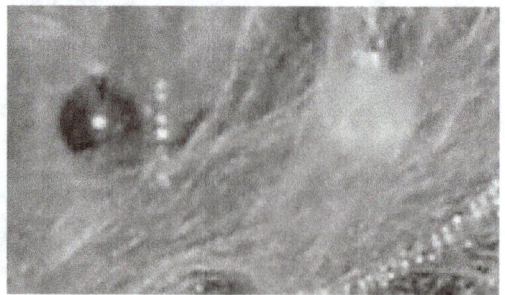

Everybody cheered and clapped and then my mom picked me up and grabbed a seat for the two of us for the gift openings.

Everybody loved it as all the gifts were given out. and I can kinda remember I loved it too. Mom had a little pile for me and I can recall there were a lot of shiny things in my pile.

From there, we hugged all the cousins and went back in the car. Mom and dad had stuff from Pop Katille and stuff for her brothers & sisters, & mom and dad at the Pop Trosk's home.

I forgot to say before that Breezie, our dog was with us at Pop Katille's. Even though we did not eat, the dog ate a lot. He ate all of the stuff the Flanders had left behind on their paper plates. Dad said he weighed a ton when he put Breezie in the car.

It was after 8:00 PM when we left for Pop Trosks house. Breezie and mom were in the back seat with me (I was in the car seat) when we went to Pop Trosks. Breezie was in mom's lap. Dad kept us all in the back to be safe.

When we got to the Trosks it took dad two or more trips to get all the stuff for the Trosk house up their steps and inside through the front door. It was not long that all my uncles and aunts and Aunt Cathy Piotroski, Aunt Hey Hey, and my Trosk cousins, Justin, Marty, Scott, and Erin were all there. Starting with Pop and Nana, here are a few pictures from that night:

Pop & Nana Trosk onlookers while Trosk festivities were in full bloom.

They all came and it was not long before we were all there. Pop had the tree and the HO train set up. Dad was holding Breezie as nobody wanted him to root for his gifts before they were all ready to celebrate.

The Marty Trosk Family & John Baron in Nana Trosk's Kitchen

We all had some refreshments and some Kielbasa from Swantkos in Nanticoke, I had my little sippy cup and mom made sure I was OK. I was the youngest one there, including Breezie. Matt and Alie would be there in future years.

Pop passed out schnorkies. Dad had to explain what they were before I could write this part. He told me that nobody would ever drink water from a schnorkie glass because there would not be much water.

Eventually, I understood. Pop Trosk gave his toast, and immediately sang Silent night. As always, he was weeping as were many adults when he finished. Then he ran the train. Breezie was getting fidgety when Pop Trosk ran the train.

Then Trosk Pop called Breezie and just like the year before, he found his three squeak toys and everybody began to call out names and eventually everybody had their gifts in front of them and they opened them to their delight.

Breezie was in the corner with his three squeak toys loving every minute of the Christmas celebration. Every now and then Pop Trosk would slip Breezie a piece of kielbasa. They had both the fresh and smoked varieties from Uncle Stan's buddy's Swantko's Butcher shop.

Everybody was enjoying the gifts they got as were Pop and Nana (Arline) Trosk. Mom opened my gifts with me and I remember there were toys and they seemed all shiny. It was nice.

Eventually it was time to go.

When we got back to Cummings Street, mom said she then told me all about Santa and that good things would happen over-night when Santa came. Dad and mom tucked me in and I fell right asleep for the whole night.

No, after learning what they were, I can say that I did not have a schnorkie while looking forward to my seventh birthday. No, my shoulders had not begun to change yet, either.

If asked on Christmas day, if I had any dreams on Christmas Eve, now I suspect I might have gotten some applause if I had said that I had visions of sugar plums dancing in my head. But, to be honest, I am not sure that I did.

I do know that it was such a nice night that I smiled all the while I slept and I woke up with a big smile on my face.

That morning before I knew what was going on, Dad had me in his arms. He changed me (We don't have to talk about that) and he brought me downstairs. Mom had a camera and got a lot of great pictures of my arrival on Christmas day.

Mom told me the story of this, my first Christmas, many times since. I was a lucky baby. My brother and sister also were lucky babies as I saw the love mom and dad gave then on their first Christmases.

Dad put me down that morning on the living room rug right by a pile of gifts. Mom kept snapping pictures. In the pictures that I remember I was in the middle of all the gifts.

Here is a picture of Dad on Christmas day coming down the open staircase.

To mom and dad, they told me I was their best gift ever. Of course, that was before Mortrock and Katers showed up over the next several years.

All gifts this first Christmas appeared to be toys and they were all shiny and happy looking. I wish I could remember what they were. I don't know if this is that Christmas look by the tree but it was one of them.

The great look under the platform under the Christmas Tree

Though I do not recall getting it on Christmas day, I do know that year I got a magnetic blackboard and a couple sets of letters and numbers that would stick to the board. Throughout the year of 1981 and even 1982, I played with that board all the time.

Mom said that before too long, because dad and Pop Trosk were always showing me numbers and letters, I began to count early and I was able to form small words like dog and cat. I remember loving stuff like that.

After we opened all of my gifts from Santa, mom told me that I noticed two more piles by the tree. They were from mom to dad and from dad to mom. We left them there and I did not complain.

Mom then picked me up and walked me to the kitchen where she placed me in my high chair for my Christmas breakfast. I am sure it was some great Gerber product, which I had all the time and which I recall I loved very much. I was about seven months old at the time.

Mom and dad carried me down to Pop Katille and Grandma Biddie's house for Christmas dinner at noon sharp. They lived about seven doors down from us. We had a nice Turkey Dinner with Pop Katille and Grandma Biddie and Uncle Joe who lived there. Breezie always got his share from Biddie. Dad's sisters and brother Ed had their own places to be and were not there for this dinner.

We stayed awhile watching football and then we walked back home, and mom told me I was tired so she put me up for an afternoon nap in my crib.

The crib was in the only bed room that was decorated pink. Four years later it became my sister Kater's room after Mortrock got his crib there a couple years before her arrival.

Dad longed for an office but the house was too small so dad used the dining room table to do his at home IBM work. Later on Christmas afternoon , I think mom and dad took a nap as they too were filled and tuckered out from the night before.

In addition to Pop and Grandma Biddie, Pop and Nana Trosk always had a big Turkey dinner for Christmas day at about 6:00 PM. Even Breezie was tired so he slept on the cool kitchen floor. Mom got me up and got me all dressed up again for Christmas at the Trosks.

Pop Trosk was watching football and Dad joined him in the living room. Nana set up the dining-room which did not happen often. When Nana called everybody to eat, the Trosks all found seats at the big table. Mom and I were with them.

All of mom's brothers and sisters were there with their wives and husbands.

Pop Trosk and dad ate dinner in the kitchen. Pop Trosk had come in from visiting friends at the Legion. Dad really loved being with Pop Trosk. Everybody had a great time and the turkey was absolutely delicious.

Because there were giblets in the dressing, Dad had an extra wad of potatoes instead of stuffing. Dad was never a giblet guy.

When Grandma Biddie passed away, mom and dad began to make dinner ourselves for Thanksgiving and Christmas, Dad always boiled the giblets for Breezie and the dog smacked his lips as he consumed every morsel. Pop Katille then began to have a turkey dinner for the family on Christmal Eve.

Because Christmas Eve had been such a late night this year, everybody was tired. Santa was good to everybody as I recall mom saying. It was now very dark. We left the Trosks with another pile of gifts that we had left behind the night before. .

When we got home, mom and dad tucked me in almost right away. I went right to sleep. Mom said there was a ton of food in the house and dad said that he gained at least five pounds over the holidays.

I remember them taking me to a lot of houses over the holidays. Nana and Pop Trosk came down the house and Pop Katille and Grandma Biddie joined us to bring in the new year.

The lady on the other side of the Zabola;s Kaye Pavlov, came over also and joined us for New Year's Eve. Barbara and Joseph Zabola also were there. We played Guy Lombardo music and had some champagne. Mom still loves champagne.

We named Mrs. Pavlov--Good Kaye because she was a good lady and it sounded good. On New Year's Eve,. the two pops and two nanas, mom and dad, and Good Kaye and Barbara Zabola danced to dad's stereo by the homemade bar in the in the gold room and when somebody spinned Good Kaye, she always went *whee!*

It was a great New Years' Eve. The next day it was a great New Years' Day. Mom said that Dad watched every bowl game there was on New Years' Day while most of the time I was napping. Mom took care of me that day and every day.

It was January 1, 1981. This was my first holiday of my second calendar year alive. I was about to learn that there were a lot of other holidays and a great summer in which to look forward. I did.

Chapter 8 St. Patrick's Day and Easter 1981

I was soon talking and walking

St. Patrick's Day came like clockwork, two and a half months after New Year's Day. It was what mom called, another cold winter. Dad was away for several weeks as he liked to get his IBM technical education classes out of the way early in the year. He had classes in Texas and in Rochester, Minnesota.

By St. Patrick's Day, the weather had warmed up quite a bit. On Saturday, March 14, 1981, Wilkes-Barre City held their annual St. Patrick's Day Parade.

Mom and Dad parked in the Station Restaurant's parking lot and pushed my stroller to South Main Street to see the parade. It was great. We had a wonderful view of all the great action.

They had dressed me warm so I felt very good and every now and then somebody would throw some soft candy, which my parents would swoop up and give me a taste.

They had everything in this parade. I had never heard or seen bagpipers, but they filled the streets of Wilkes-Barre on this Saturday afternoon for the city's second annual St. Patrick's Day Parade. The most recent parade in 2019 was the 39th.

There were dozens of floats and marching bands from all the schools and a place called The Irem Temple.

They all entertained the crowd, including me, and mom and dad and there were about 500 participants and perhaps more in this great event. I was amazed at the huge Fire Engines. It was my first parade.

Mom and dad took me, Mortrock and Katers when they came along to many such parades, including the Santa Claus parade at Christmas time.

It seemed like just an instant and we were back in the car headed home. Dad made a combination of corned beef brisket and ham and cabbage and potatoes and we enjoyed that meal on Sunday. Dad still makes a great St. Patrick's day dinner plus he buys about five dinners at St. Patrick's Church.

The next big family holiday was on Easter. Pop Katille had a big chicken dinner every Sunday in which all the Katilles were invited including me. Pop Trosk had a similar dinner which we all attended. His was roast beef and chicken soup.

Most often Uncle Marty and Aunt Cathy and Marty, Erin, and Scott were the only Trosks who made it to the Trosks for Sunday dinner besides mom and dad.

Easter was not just a regular Sunday but until Nana Biddie passed away, the dinners were the same. Then, instead of cooking, we went up Aunt Marie's and pop Katille took all the Katille's to KFC After dinner.

For over fifty years now, after the Katille dinner later in the afternoon, my mom put on a very nice Easter Egg hunt for as many as fifteen kids – all my cousins and some neighbors… all the little ones and the biggers were invited too.

Yes, from when she was eighteen years old and little Marty Trosk was just born, mom ran an Easter Egg hunt. In the early days, it was always in Pop Trosk's big yard on Hillside Street in Wilkes-Barre.

This year after dinner was no different. Pop Katille and all the Katille cousins all came to the hunt. It kept getting bigger every year. I was eleven months old and could walk by then, but I still needed dad to help me collect my bag of eggs. Fun!

Mom also walked with me in my first Easter Egg Hunt and I found over twenty aluminum wrapped chocolate Easter Eggs. The Easter Bunny had wrapped them tight.

Everybody loved it. Mom gave the winner a really big bunny. I forget who won the event in my first Easter Egg hunt but I can remember we all loved it. What a great time for kids. It sure looked like the adults were having fun also.

Chapter 9 The Summer of 1981

The cousins almost swimming underwater

This was dad's first year in which he had to get the Muskin pool set up for the summer without Mike Kurilla and Romy Shedleski being there for him.

Both the Mike Kurilla Family and the Ken Evans family were still living down the street so dad he had all the help that he needed right on our street if he needed a hand. But, by and large, he got it done himself.

Dad said it was lots easier than he had thought. He first took off the cover and unfortunately, it had developed a hole over the winter so the dirty water and the leaves on the top of the cover seeped into the pool.

Dad had brought the pool level down below the skimmer in the fall when he put on the cover. This was to make sure the plastic skimmer would not freeze during the winter and then bust.

So, his first step was to hook up the pool pump and the sand filter again to keep the water in the pool. Then he began to fill the pool with the hose.

In about eight hours, the pool was high enough that dad could turn on the pump. When he did, everything worked. But, the water was very dirty.

The next thing dad did was to get the leaf skimmers attached to the handles so he and mom could work on getting the wet, rotting leaves out.

When that was done, dad set the filter to waste and while the hose was putting water in, the murky water that was taken from the bottom was spilling out onto the ground. After that the pool was pretty clear. Dad refilled it about a foot a few times to keep the dirty water elimination going along.

Dad brought the water level up, added a little sand to the filter, and then he ran the pump, backwashing periodically. Each day for two to three days, it kept getting clearer.

In three days it was ready for swimmers, But it was just the second week in May and it was still too cold.

Something great happened in the Spring time. My new buddy Mary, who was my age, came over with her mom, Barbara. She came with her brother Dave and her sister Kim and sister Dawn. The Zabolas were a great family.

I got to know the Zabola's first because they lived so close and we liked them all. When Mortrock was born and about a year old in 1983, Mr. Zabola took a real liking to him and he helped him learn to swim.

I was with all the Zabola kids the first warm day of 1981 around Memorial day. Nobody knew how to swim.

Mom was in the pool with me on my first day. She had me in a little ducky inner-tube and she had inflatable arms that were called swimmies at the time.

It did not take long for me to be able to navigate the pool without mom holding on. By the end of May, on my birthday, May 28th, I was a whole one-year old.

Despite how good I got, all summer long, mom never let me in the pool by myself. Looking back, I understand why.

Dave and Kim were tall enough that they could stand on their toes and be out of the water. Dawn was a little bigger than me and Mary was just a little smaller. Mary also needed the tube & the swimmies.

The Zabolas had an old pool in their yard that was not in good shape. Dad said they did not use that pool much. The whole Zabola family were in our pool more than we were, so in just a short while, they got rid of their old pool.

I remember that it looked unusable anyway. There was no patching it. Mr. Zabola dismantled it piece by piece. It took a few weeks before it was all done and out of their yard.

When he had all the metal from the pool in one place, he put it in his trunk and sold it to Solomon's Junk Yard a few blocks away for a few bucks.

With the money he got, he bought some nectar and he made a great fondue for everybody to enjoy. Our families often celebrated with nectar together. Dad made sure that Mr. Zaboloa knew that he could use our pool anytime.

Mr. Zabola became a regular in our pool for the rest of the summer. He was a wonderful man. His wife Barbie was a wonderful lady.

She and my mom, Patricia "Petrinka" Katille became best friends. There was often nectar, cold and gold, by the pool in the summer of 1981.

Evacuate the Pool!

I was told that I pressed the edges for mom. She wanted sometimes to not be checking diapers all the time yet she had to when I was in the pool. When I got into the pool with mom, she told me later that I had a bad habit of doing my habit right out of the diaper and into the pool.

Mom would be holding me. While she was holding me, I made my habit. Then everybody would have to evacuate the pool for an hour. Mom got the strainer and another bottle of bleach and put it in to sanitize the pool before letting anybody go back in.

Before such an excretory event, apparently, I would always hold onto mom just a little tighter.

That would end the swimming but after an hour the rest of the kids and Mr. Zabola were right back in the pool. As I said Mom never let me in the pool alone. She was afraid for my safety and she knew that she had to watch out for diaper-doo.

My dad, Brian Sr. or Brunick as his dad often called him, was most often at work at IBM during the daytime hours.

Sometimes he went away for a week or several days for technical seminars. So, he was not with us all the time in the pool.

Dad loved to sing songs in the pool and we would all join him. His favorite song when swimming that first year was the two-line squirrel song which I wrote down for you a while ago.

Everybody enjoyed singing it with him. Dad loved the pool and he loved being with me in the pool. Here is the song again in case you forgot:

This is not a Squirrel Pool
This is a Whirlpool

I would like to jump ahead a few years in this story just for a little while as we are talking about singing. This is a little story about my brother. He was not born until December 30 of this year, 1981. It was not long after he was born that dad and mom decided to name him Mortrock. He was a definite madcap. He was always into something.

I bring him up now because after a few years, we also sang Mortrock's two songs in the pool with dad. He created one of them when in his car seat with Nana Skippo while on a trip to Boston to see Aunt Sue and Uncle Mitch and he created the other at the Stanton Street Playground while being pushed on the swings.

The Car seat song had one word "Lo." Mortrock sang it the best. It went like this

Lo Lo Lo Lo,
Lo Lo Lo Lo
Lo Lo Lo Lo,
Lo Lo Lo Lo.

Sometimes Mortrock would go on with additional verses using the same word but most of the time, it was just those four lines. Dad and mom really got a kick out of that song.

The song from the Stanton Street Playground that Mortrock created had a few more words. He called it his bumble bee song and every time he was on the swings, he would sing it with a very happy tone.

Bumble Bee, Who's There? Bumble Bee
Bumble Bee, Who's There? Bumble Bee

Mom and dad and I loved hearing him sing that song too and so we loved it when he would sing it in the pool. When he did, we would all sing along with him. It made us all smile. Sometimes when Morty sang, dad would say we were all watching *The Morty Show*.

One more Morty story before I go back to the pool and the summer of 1981. When we were not in the pool in the summer of 1983, we were either just getting up, going to bed, or it was raining out.

Mom set my letter and number board up in the hallway right outside Dad's office, especially when it was raining.

When Mortrock came, he and I were always together at the top of the steps.

Morty had real curly hair so much so that Uncle Joe called him the mad professor. Mom could not get herself for a year or more to get him a haircut so that explains that. She thought it was so cute.

Anyway, I would love to spell words and by the time Mortrock was around, I could form interesting words with my letters using the magnetic board. I loved it.

Dad found out Mortrock, who from day one was a great athlete, also liked the letters and numbers from the board.

Dad was coming up the front steps, probably to go to the bathroom as there was just one set of stairs.

At the bottom he saw a few letters and numbers and he figured I had dropped them when building words on the magnetic board.

He picked them up for me and as he proceeded up the steps, on most steps he found a letter or a number or two. Then he looked up the steps.

Mortrock was right in front of the gate at the top of the steps with a letter in his hand. He took the letter and like you would skip a rock on a lake he fired the letter with his little hand and it went down the steps and hit dad in the chest.

Mortrock loved the letters and I loved the letters but when he was just a little guy, he liked to throw them and I liked to build words out of them. We love each other as brothers for sure but we are different.

This 1985 picture is Mortrock and sister Katers at Pop Trosk's house.

Back to the summer of 1981.

I hope you liked the diversion about my brother Mortrock. I have stories about my sister Katers that I will tell one day. She is very nice, smart, and a great athlete like Morty. The stork waited another two and a half years to bring her into the world.

Let me say that like Mortrock, she loved to swim and she loved to throw things. She is still a great athlete.

By the end of the summer, when I was about 15 months old, I was able to stay afloat in the pool as could Mary, my best buddy back then. Mom was always in the pool when we were in the pool and Mr. Zabola was in there a lot also. Dad would say that I could "tread water."

By the way, I looked up the definition of treading water: "Maintain an upright position in deep water by moving the feet with a walking movement and the hands with a downward circular motion." So there, I did my research.

I was the first child in the Brian W. Katille family to be able to swim. But, then again, in the summer of 1981, my brother Mortrock and sister Katers were not born yet.

I remember when mom let me go the first time without the swimmies or the duck tube. I surprised myself even. I was a little scared, I began to move my arms and legs and I was soon in the middle of the pool. I was not sinking. I was almost "swimming." Success! I was treading water. That's about as far as I got in the summer of 1981.

Chapter 10 The Fall of 1981

Mom and dad bought a queen-size bed after Poppy finished the remodeling years ago. TVs were pretty expensive then so they put a small TV set in their bedroom but they said they did not watch it very much until I came around.

When there was no need to rush up and get outside since the pool was closed, I soon was big enough that when mom got me out of the crib on Saturday mornings and ahem, after she changed me (shhh!!!), I made the big trip.

She would walk me down the small upstairs hallway to the mom and dad bedroom and she would put me between dad and her on the queen-sized bed.

We had cable tv and a remote was always handy. There were great kids shows on Saturday Morning. I know I liked Scooby Doo and of course the Smurfs. My dad liked the song about the pixies (picture shown on prior page) when we watched the Smurfs. Here is the song:

It was called "The Wartmonger Song."

It was a song sung by the three Wartmonger hunters -- Slop, Sludge, and Slime -- in a few Smurfs cartoon show episodes featuring them. Here are the lyrics:

All Three sing:
Oh, we are mighty hunters
In service to the king.
When we go hunting pixies,
We really clip their wings.

Sludge sings:
I'm Sludge the brave.

Slop sings:
I'm Slop the bold.

Slime sings:
I'm Slime the slimy thing.

All Three sing:
When we go hunting pixies,

We really clip their wings, their wings,
Their wingy-wingy-wings.

How can anybody not like that song. Dad loved it. He would sing it at breakfast time after we got up.

Speaking of breakfast, we did not see many, many shows on Saturday morning in bed because we all got hungry and dad would make panapoona. That was dad's word for pancakes. Boy, were they good.

By the fall of 1981, I remember that I could talk and walk but I could not say really big words such as calculator. Dad had a big adding machine on his "office" desk which was just a table and OK dad had no real office then. As it got colder, I was not outside as much as when the pool was going. I loved that adding machine.

By mid-September, dad had closed up the pool. He said that August was not too bad weather-wise but as soon as Labor Day came, it got too cold to swim.

Dad loved putting me on his lap as he sat in front of his new big "desk table" in his bedroom. He had bought it at the Salvation Army for $30.00. He still has it.

I guess I got pretty good with the adding machine and I could use it to add and subtract at first. I was not into multiplication or division. Dad also let me use his pocket calculator I loved the calculator. Eventually dad let me have it most of the time.

I loved the calculator, which, before I had begun to speak big words properly, I called the "kuh-shah-shun."

One time at K-Mart, mom's favorite store, we took dad's route to the toys. It passed this neat looking counter and as he was passing it, I can recall and dad loves to tell the story that I screamed out:

"kuh-shah-shun."
"kuh-shah-shun."

Dad finally noticed and took me over to see the display models of a bunch of calculators that K-Mart was selling. Wow! It was like heaven.

I did like those calculators as a little kid. Now I love music and personal computers.

I graduated from Wilkes-University with major honors and a degree in Computer Science. Now, I am a lawyer. I went to Villanova Law School and did quite well. I passed the Bar Exam the first time with a great score. That's quite a big difference from "kuh-shah-shun." to computer science. I also got the Science Award at Wilkes. It was a great honor.

So, that was the great K-Mart "kuh-shah-shun." caper. I can almost remember it. Now we are back to the story and we are about to begin the most exciting chapters of this story.

This year, 1981, was my favorite Christmas ever. It was about to be my second Christmas. Before the Christmas holidays were over and before the Christmas stuff was put down the cellar for another year. my brother Mortrock was born the day before New Years Eve.

That was the greatest. It made me nineteen months older than him. It took Katers two and a half more years to coax the stork to bring her home.

As I told you earlier in the book, the neighbors said that Mortrock and I were Irish twins. I knew we were Irish with some Polish from Mom, but I never understood the twins part. We were not twins. At least I did not think so. Here is a picture of mom, dad and Mortrock in the hospital right after Morty was born

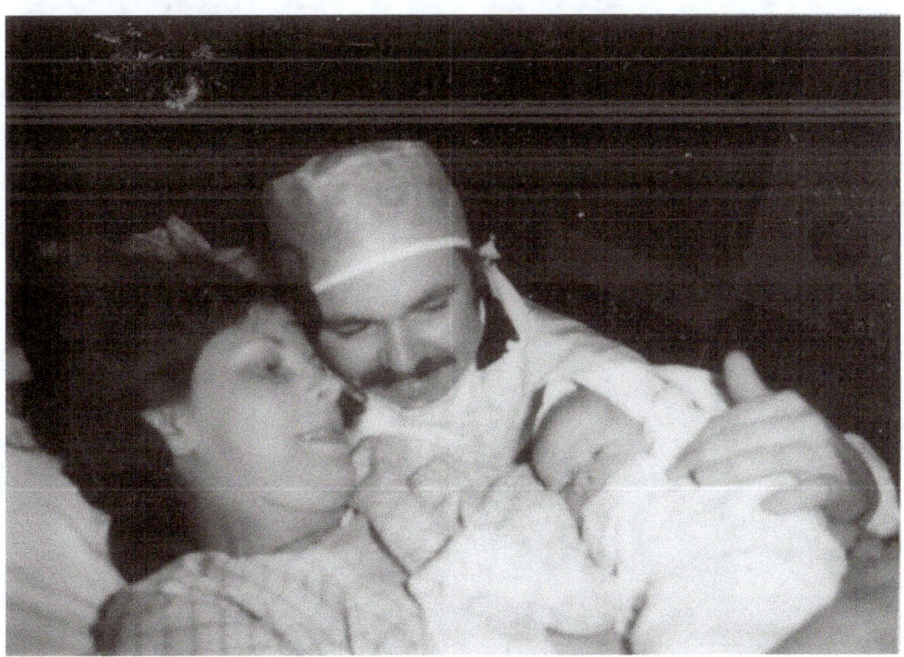

Chapter 11 Baby Brian's Second Christmas

This picture is from Christmas 1982 when Mortrock was 1 and I was 2 ½.

Christmas in 1981 was quite special as I was almost two years old and I began to notice the muscles in my back more and more. Mortrock, on the right in pic from 1982, above had come during the Christmas season 1981 on December 30.

For the longest time, all he did was sleep. At first mom and dad squeezed in a crib in the second bedroom where

Mortrock and I slept. A year or so later was when as I recall they built me my own bedroom and Morty was still in the crib in the second bedroom. I am not sure of all that.

I wondered if mom and dad could see the muscles behind my shoulders that we'll be talking about soon— but they never said anything about it.

Dad and mom helped me so much with numbers that I could not only count to ten, I could count to 100 long before Christmas that year. Dad would even drill me on counting backwards. By Christmas at 19-months, I could count from 100 backwards and that amazed both mom and dad. I thought it was easy

They had me counting for neighbors, friends and relatives. Before Christmas, mom and dad had me adding and subtracting. Sometimes they would give me more than two numbers to work with at a time. I loved numbers and letters. It was great.

In early December, Dad put up the train again and I was mesmerized looking at it as it took shape. As soon as Dad got the train and tree up, just like the year before, he brought out the transformer and taught me how to operate it.

I called the train, the Toot Toot. When Mortrock and Katers eventually were both born and they ran the train, they called it the cho-choo-woo-woo. I could walk pretty good this Christmas by then and I remember being in the living room looking for the transformer but could never find it. So, I never got to run the train without dad by my side. It was OK by me.

I had grown a lot since Christmas 1980, and was big enough that without a booster-chair, I could see the whole platform. I admit that a few times, I did reach in a couple times past the fence and I grabbed an ice skater, or a caroler or a house to get a better look.

Mom was quick even if she was not there to begin with. She would catch me and tell me not to do that and then she would put the figure back where it belonged. She never yelled at me.

Mr. Christian's Platform

Before Christmas Eve, dad and mom took me to the Christians up in Dupont PA. Dad worked with Mr. Christian and he had a great platform for Christmas that took two rooms.

There were at least four different working trains on the platform plus he had planes and helicopters that when I squinted, I could not see the wires holding them above the platform in a few different places.

Now I realize that the wires to the planes were connected to the ceiling but that Newswatch 16 chopper looked so real. When the four trains were running at the same time, across all the great scenes Mr. Christian had built, it was like a winter wonderland and the automated areas and the running helicopter made it all so real. For the first time in my short life, I began to wish that I could fly.

If I could not be an airplane or helicopter pilot then I decided I wanted to be an engineer on one of those great trains of Mr. Christian's. I wanted to learn how to drive the train at full size rather than being shrunk down to train platform size.

As neat as it was to see the trains go through mountain after mountain and the helicopters looking so real over the different platform worlds Mr. Christian had created, I had at first missed the most interesting part of the platform.

At first, I did not see it but then, there it was. He had created an area in the platform confines in which birds were flying from one spot to another. They might have been holograms. I don't know. They looked real in miniature.

If they were not real, it sure looked like they were. I do not know to this day how he did it but it looked like the birds were flying from one of his remote platform worlds to another and back.

There were at least ten birds of differing types such as eagles and ravens and crows and there was what looked to be a giant dinosaur bird. Wow. I did not know how I had first missed that.

Mr. Christian had the best Christmas display I had ever seen even though the trains were not LGB like dad's. After he walked us around to where the birds were seemingly actually flying, there was a small cubby hole corner in the room and he took us there.

The platform went through the whole corner. The paint was darker and Mr. Christian had the lights dim when we got close. I can't believe what we saw.

My dad's friend had studied the Pterosaurs also called Pterodactyl, which is a dinosaur that can fly like an airplane. I don't think I could have spelled any of those things if mom had not helped me when I was writing this. It was real. Actually, for me it was scary. I was glad dad was there with me on this visit.

Mr. Christian was very talented and was seemingly able to superimpose objects into a real setting and then make them move. The good news for all of us was that these dinosaur birds, and there were too many of them to not be afraid, were platform sized, and not life-sized. It scared me anyway.

While we were all watching, like as if the movie had changed, out of nowhere, a young boy appeared with a huge pair of wings. He was platform sized also and he was flying close to the new section of the platform that we were observing. The boy had wings coming out of the back of his shoulders by what we can call the wing bone. Wow!

He approached the flying dinosaurs like he was not afraid. When he got there, he stopped all the flurrying by landing and then he opened his huge wings all the way. Immediately all the flying in this last world stopped on the platform. Even the birds.

Mr. Christian spoke then and everything seemed more like it was happening just on the platform rather than alive on the platform. I got the feeling the tour was winding down and it was. It had finished. But I could not see mom and dad—just Mr. Christian. They were talking to Mr. Christian's mom and dad while he was talking to me.

He was a fine man and it showed through all he did. He loved showing us all of his two room Christmas platform. Mom and dad loved it too as it was early January and she had baby Mortrock with us at the Christians. But, right now it was just Mr. C., and I as he wrapped up the tour.

He asked me if he could say a few words to me when the platform visit was clearly over and the birds appeared to be still and on rocks and the young boy, who had been flying was standing as a figure on a big rock resting on the platform. I said sure. Dad trusted him.

Mr. Christian got serious but calmed me down with the gentle tone of his voice. He asked me about the two sets of muscles in my upper back. He knew I had them. He told me this was a sign that I would be blessed with more gifts over the years that very few people ever receive. He cautioned me not to be frightened when I learned more about the gifts.

He somehow knew that until I had seen the Newswatch 16 helicopter and the planes and the birds and the flying dinosaurs and the flying young man who commanded the dinosaurs within the different worlds that I had no idea of what flying was like. I told him that I got a sense that I was meant to fly but I could not explain it.

I told him that I was in awe as more things kept appearing on his platform. I admitted I had in that short while developed a love of flight and hoped that one day, I too could fly in a helicopter, a plane or be like a bird or the flying dinosaur. I hoped to be able to fly as a full-sized human being like the boy on the rock.

I was not yet two years old and all this was happening to me. I had not yet reached the age of reason and yet, I was reasoning things that should never have been in my life.

Mr. Christian told me to fear not that his mission in life was to help me and others like me to understand their gifts and to understand why we were so blessed.

He also told me that there was an obligation that those of us with these gifts would have in life as we got older in life. In other words, whoever had such gifts had to use them for good purposes or give them up.

I was so young, yet he knew he could speak to me. He cautioned me not to tell my dad what we had just discussed about my gifts and he then said that in the rest of his words, he would tell me of the greatest part of the gifts that I would receive as I got older.

When I reached seven years old the transition would be complete and then, after I took my first flight by myself, that I would be able to tell my dad and mom about what God had given to me.

He explained that the muscles on my back under the shoulder which all formed the human wing bone were the buds of wings that would develop over the next few years. Though it seemed now like just muscles because I was just approaching 20 months of age, it was the beginning of a cluster of muscle and bones and tendons also called sinews that would become two perfectly symmetrical wings. They would grow in proportion to the size of the wings on the young man whose vision I saw on the platform.

I was amazed.

He told me that the spirits from heaven over time would be communicating with me and they would every now and then give me special assignments to help humans in trouble or who had special needs.

My wings, he said would pull into my body and seemingly dissipate when they were not in use. I would have the wings until I was twelve years old and then according to plan, they would fold back into my body and would become non-functional and basically disappear.

Yet, he also said that possibly well after turning twelve, the forces that be might need me again, and that would be possible.

He told me that all of the body architectural changes necessary would be made as men were not built to fly. My changed body would be able to include large wings of major strength in my human body.

This full process would be completed when I was seven years old but at all times, they would be invisible to the naked eye. When I went to the doctor, even he would not see how different internally from all others that my body had become.

Only when my wings became visible in pre-flight or during flight or post-flight temporarily would there be any trace of the wonder that would be hidden in my changed body.

There would be very few people, and only special people would ever know about them and he cautioned me again not to discuss them or about our conversation with anybody.

He said never to take a picture of the metamorphosis as it would scare people. He also told me that he was going to be married and would be moving down in my neighborhood in Wilkes-Barre in about a year or so.

He said everything would be OK even though I would not see him again for several years until little Katers was born and my dad and mom would bring me over to his house close to our neighborhood to see his train set again.

Just then, mom and dad and his mom and dad called out for us as we were in the second platform room. Mr. Christian said that we were just about finished talking and he led me around so I did not step on any of the platform figures.

Soon, we joined up again with mom and dad and Baby Mortrock where we left them all when we went to the other side of the platform. What a day!

What an experience. Though I always remembered that this had happened to me, I never shared it with anybody and thankfully, it was not always on my mind. Thus, I continued to lead a normal live as a very young boy. When I read about what I have written now, it is almost unbelievable. But, I lived it.

It was just a few days after the new year and I had felt something that I could not explain. The Christmas Eve and Christmas before the beginning of this new year was just like the year before though I don't remember much about 1980.

Let me go back to Christmas Eve for just a bit as mom just found this picture from Pop Katille's home on Hillside Street. I thought you'd like to see it.

Grandma Biddie had put the Angel Hair on just like the year before and then we got our gifts. It was great. We all had something to drink and then we went up to Pop and Nana Trosk's. We were not the first there but not the last either. Nobody knew what was going to happen at the Christians in a few weeks.

Aunt Mary always helped at Pops.
Looks like an ahem, diaper, in her hand?

Aunt Sue was normally last to arrive at Pop Trosks, which happened later that evening after she came in from Boston. Same this year. Pop shared some schnorkies with everybody, sang Silent Night. It made everybody cry again and then he ran the train for me and Breezie. Breezie loved the train and his squeak toys.

Christmas #2 in the Morning

This was still 1981 but I wanted to close out Christmas because I was not sure how long the Mr. Christian story was going to take when I told that before this. So, here goes. This great chapter is almost finished.

In the fall, we were not sure whether Mortrock or Katers would be a boy or not but the stork must have told mom something as there was definitely a crib for Mortrock when he showed up.

Mom and dad said on Christmas day, "Merry Christmas Briney," and they each gave me a big hug. I was 19 months old on Christmas day and in a week or so I would be at Mr. Christian's house. Om said I said: "Do you think Santa was here already, mom ?"

Mom got the camera out and we began our trip down the stairs. She was snapping pictures all the while. The day and the night were magnificent. The platform on Cummings Street looked just about the same was it did in the 1980 pictures.

Chapter 12 After Christmas 1981—A New Brother!

Two Great Dinners

Christmas was on a Friday this year, so we had a long weekend. Dad had taken off the whole Christmas season to the end of the year. Because mom was "with child" during the holiday seasons, Dad expected a new little person to be living at 54 Cummings Street by the end of the holy season.

Anticipating that he would have to help out a lot when the stork brought the new baby, Dad had told his employer, IBM, that if the baby showed up during the holidays, he would be taking two weeks-vacation afterwards nd then he would be taking every Wednesday off for five more weeks.

Dad did not bother making plans to go out on New Years' Eve this year with Mom or to have Good Kaye come over. He figured the stork would come on New Year's Eve. But, asked later, he said he was hoping for more earlier than later.

On December 29, mom was feeling funny. Nana and Pop Katille and Nana and Pop Trosk came to our house to be with me. Dad took mom to the hospital.

Nothing happened on the 29th but on December 30th, the day before New Year's Eve, the grandparents got the call. The stork had brought the new baby and it was a boy. His name was Kevin. Just a day later dad and mom had changed his name to Mortrock. I was 19 months older than this little man/

Here is a nice picture of Mortrock and Mom and me by the tree the next day after he came home. He is my baby brother.

It was pretty busy in the house all week as we enjoyed Mortrock and the tree and the toys and the choo choo train. I was hoping it would never end. But as we all know, it did end. Life goes on

Chapter 13 Life Goes On!

A few extra pictures.

My second Christmas season on Cummings street saw the stork bring me a baby brother (Mortrock) and then in about two and a half years, that same stork (I think) brought me a baby sister (Katers. It was wonderful. Now I know why Adam needed Eve to complete his life. We all need good friends and relatives, boys and girls, and good people to love.

As I grew older, I was much happier having Mortrock and Katers and Mary and Dawn in my life than all the wonder I experienced with the Tree, the Toys, the train and all of the great sights and sounds.

What a great life.

Lots of pictures captured the essence of these holidays.

On this page, you will find a picture of the most wonderful lady in my life. I am sure Mortrock and Katers and dad feel the same. In the picture, below, holding Katers, you will find mom (Is she not simply beautiful – dad was so lucky!) then Mortrock (left) and Brian (me-left).

It was the second-last year that we lived on Cummings street. We would be moving the following year. Isn't mom beautiful? Wow! Mom says that's why all the Katille kids are so cute.

Though the picture below is not very clear and I have shown it once before in this book, I put it in this story because it shows my dad and how thrilled he was to be the father of the Katille Kids, including Katers, Mortrock, & Me. Here is a picture of Me and Mortrock and Dad. He liked wearing jeans along with a sport coat that he always called his stomping jacket.

Katers was born in 1984 but the picture on the above page is from 1985 as Katers was born November 12, 1984. She was less than two months old when she made it through the holiday last year as you can see in Mom's great picture in the open stairway on Cummings Street

For Mortrock and my first Christmas together when I was three and he was one; mom actually sewed "little men" "suits by hand. Dad could not believe how nice they were. What love!!!

Look at pictures of Mortrock when you have a chance. Even I love the little man's hair when I see it in these early pictures. I bet that mom sewed Katers' little outfit that she wore in this picture below. Mom was and is the greatest.

Dad loved that mom sewed such wonderful outfits for us so much that one year, he gave a special present to Mom. He put a huge red bow on a huge box. Mom loved it. It was a brand-new Singer Sewing Machine and it was already mounted in a desk unit to make it easier for mom to sew if she wished. She's looking right at it in this picture below:

Mom and dad were well known by our cousins for throwing great kids' parties. In the circa 1982 picture on the next page, there are a ton of wonderful little ones without Katers, who was not born yet. They are the wonderful Katille and Trosk cousins that I talk about in the stories.

Uncle Joe on the very left front – Uncle Bucko's Trestle Table

Now, this is the same handsome uncle Joe holding Mortrock in the picture below. My brother Mortrock's favorite cousin in the early years was Tara. She is uncle Joe and Aunt Diane's baby daughter. No Colleen yet! Tara and Mortrock are the same age. They have always been best of buddies. I think that is Aunt Di holding Tara below. That's Dr. J on far right front of the table.

A while ago—Unlce Joe, Mortrock, Tara and the "invisible" Auntie Di.

If this were a cartoon, I would now say That's All Folks! For now, that's how it is.

How could I not turn out OK when I had all these great relatives to help me through life? Isn't life great?

Chapter 14 Another Visit with the Wizard

Rendering of me (Brian) as a teenager with wings showing

No folks, this is not a picture of me, because I was told to take no pictures. There were no cell phones back then even if I wanted to take a selfie. Huge car-phones were the portable phones back then. Ironically, ten years after this year in this story, **1997** was when Radio Shack started selling sprint pcs cell phones. It was amazing and expensive.

Technology chips were helping make everything smaller. The combination of the dramatic improvement in service (digital technology plus very small cells) plus the cheap, approachable, everyman manner of selling the phones at a lowest common denominator store like Radio Shack, that really did the trick.

I could have found the technology in later years but it was long before before it was readily available and cheap enough to buy. Besides, I had promised not to disclose my great gifts.

Nonetheless, there are a number of friends and relatives, and even my mom, who now look at this picture who, when they look closely at the face in the picture, they swear that it is my face. But, it is not me. Close yes, but no cigar!

I will say that I never had to fly without having a special invisible harness built inside of me that permitted me to be fully clothed on the top and the bottom—unlike the picture I picked to show how the wings would look. There was definitely some ongoing magic going on there. Nobody ever saw me except once, and I will tell you about that in the next chapter.

I did agree for this picture to be represented here because it is almost perfect in the way it represents my wings except for one thing. My wings take up about twice the space and this would be seen with an accurate photograph. However, this photo does give the right impression so I am ok with it.

Growing Up

I always had a great life and even now that my time with wings was supposed to have passed, my life is still wonderful. My mom and dad are still alive and in their early seventies and they both have said that if it weren't for a bit of arthritis, they'd still feel just like kids.

Isn't that great. They gave my brother and sister and I, a great life and the best news is that our lives continue. The active period with the wings in retrospect was just a great add-on.

In December, 1986, with the Christian family living just a few blocks away from us, mom and dad had contact with them early in the month at Schiels Market, our neighborhood store. They asked if we would come over for another train and platform visit because they knew how much we enjoyed it when they lived in Dupont.

My parents said, "yes." And, so between Christmas and New Years dad arranged for us to go check out the Christian household's Christmas train platform again. I could not wait.

I began to remember some of the wonder of our last visit. I felt like something big had happened and was finishing up in my body and I was right. Would Mr. Christian tell me more. We'll know soon.

The more I remembered about that visit, the more I began to think that possibly Mr. Christian was a magical wizard or even more than that. Otherwise most of this did not make sense to me.

I bet he was a wizard or something approved by God, but you would never know it. Other than his gifts with his own platform, you would never know he could do all those magical things as well as make secret predictions about me and my wings.

Well OK, I believed that soon I would have real wings and I would be able to really fly. But, nothing is done until it is done as dad always says. And besides, I had no idea how that would work out with my regular life which, quite frankly. I loved.

Mr. Christian had gotten married since the last time we had met. He and Mrs. Christian, (I forget her first name so the wings did not affect my memory) now had a baby boy who was a bit younger than Katers.

Billie Jr. was not able to walk yet. Katers was walking but her steps were gingerly and not very sure as I recall.

Mortrock, my little brother, of course, was not only walking, he was playing whiffle ball and hard ball (T-ball) with us and boy could he whack a ball for a little guy.

Mom and dad told me I was tall for my age. Eventually, I grew to be six foot three inches tall—almost six foot-four. I don't feel that big now but I am.

I remember the day that we went to see the train setup at the Christians in 1986.. It was two days before Mortrock's fifth birthday—December 28. I was six years old and would turn seven on May 28, 1987.

Mortrock and I played T-ball that summer year for the first time. We had moved to South Wilkes-Barre on Gates Street. I was almost too old to play in the league but I got in.

After we went to Sunday Mass, we went right to the Christian home. Mr. Christian opened the door with

Mrs Christian. She was holding little Billie. She immediately took us to their dining room table where they had a load of cookies and milk and other drinks for us.

She is a very good baker. Dad had a coffee and mom had a tea. Billie was buzzing around in his walker which had a front tray on it. He was eating cookies too. His walker looked like the one in the picture below:

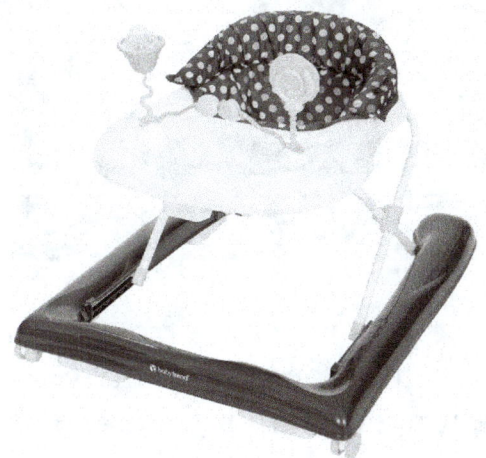

After the treats, Mr. Christian led us down the basement steps and this is just about what we saw. Wow!

From this view as we came from down the basement steps, his platform got a little skinny on the right side before it opened up into a second room on the right.

It was all bigger than the setup we had seen when they lived in Dupont with big Bill's mom and dad. In the second room in Dupont, Mr. C. had the planes and helicopters etc.

One little diversion about platform trains, please. I was riding my bike in our new neighborhood later this year when a man named Carl Naessig Jr., the best insurance guy in Wilkes-Barre helped me fix a flat tire. He was taking out some old green soiled platform paper to the garbage area.

After he fixed my flat, I told him the paper looked like platform paper and he was surprised I knew. I told him I loved trains and he asked me if I wanted to see his display. Mrs Naessig was also very nice and she came down the basement to see my reaction. They ran this huge set of trains for me. They were the heavy Lionel—beautiful. They got a big "yeah" from me for sure.

My dad told me how to spell Naessig but first he had checked in with Carol Anstett and John Anstett from the neighborhood. They assured dad that the spelling was correct—end of diversion.

In Mr. Christian's new platform set, he had three huge Lionel transformers to control the trains and a bunch of other accessories that controlled the switches and the lights etc. It was awesome to say the least. I am thirty-nine years old now as I write this and I still love looking at that great picture above.

Mortrock and Katers were there too and we all got to run the train. The Christians brought little Billy down in his walker and he was buzzing around between the rooms enjoying himself.

Mr. Christian took each of us, one by one and he showed us how to operate two of the big trains that were on the outside. After he showed us each, he let us take turns operating the whole set up for about five minutes at a time. First me, then Mortrock, and then Katers got to operate this whole menagerie. We all felt like big shots.

The train and the bird section were there but the small boy with the wings was not there nor were any of the figures flying as I remembered from the first time we saw the display. I did not say anything about them ever but I remembered them. In fact I had not told anybody, even Mortrock anything since our first visit.

It was different this time but still fun. After more than an hour of our operating it all, dad and mom said we had to get back for our Sunday dinner at Pop Katille's house.

So, we all started up the steps for our coats and to leave. I was on the last steps looking at the platform as Mr. Christian was shutting off all the lights and power.

He caught up with me quickly as I was daydreaming and he stopped me and spoke to me. I stopped when I was almost at the top. Everybody else was gone to the first floor. Mr. Christian said "Hello Brian. It was like he did when we first came in and then he reminded me of our last talk about the wings.

I told him that my wings were pretty big now and I had seen them but they retracted in my back when I was not thinking about them. He told me that was normal and that I had just about six months to wait before they were full sized and I could actually begin to use them.

He said something else which got me to thinking that I might be seeing a lot of Mr. Christian over the next couple years. Very softly he said to me that when I am out enjoying my new ability to fly, to stop over his house so he could talk to me and see how I looked.

He told me that before we went home, he was going to keep Dad a little while longer to explain what changes were to happen to me. I was not seven years old yet so I think that was good. He said when dad came out to the car to leave, he would know the whole story.

We then continued up the steps and mom had my coat. We were at the front door before I knew it and we said our good-bys. Mom opened up our car and let us all in. It was just like Mr. Christian had said. He kept dad with him for a while. While we were in the car, mom seemed concerned that dad did not come right out.

In fact, Dad did not come out for about fifteen minutes and we were getting later for dinner at Pop and Biddie Katille's. Eventually dad came out and mom chided him a little for keeping us all waiting.

He said he was sorry and told her he would tell her about the recipes Mrs. Christian had given him for her and that she (Mrs. Christian) was going to send him a letter with more Christmas recipes.

That made mom happy. Dad looked at me and winked. I knew he knew and dad was very happy that day so I knew it would all be OK when I turned seven years of age—the age of reason.

"Hey Mortrock, in just six months I will be seven years old. Dad says this is the age of reason."

Chapter 15 The Day of the Big Birthday

Without telling secrets, I bet you can't find me in this picture

First Communion

Two weeks before my combination First Communion Sunday and seventh birthday party scheduled for May 31, 1987—a party that mom and dad had been promising me since Thanksgiving 1986, I received my actual first communion. After Confession and Communion, I never felt closer to God.

It was on May 17. My actual birthday came every year on May 28. This year, it was a Thursday. My combination party was scheduled for the following Sunday, the 31st.

It seemed like all the kids in my class at St. Boniface School had parties on May 17, the day of our First communion. There were two other guys and a girl whose parties were not on the 17th. All the kids' parents invited all the kids in the class to all the parties on the 17th of May.

The moms and dads of the other three classmates who were not having a party on May 17 right after the First Communion, scheduled their parties on May 24, one week after First Communion Sunday, and coincidentally, just one week before my combination party.

I was able to attend all of their parties and just about everybody's party on the 17th. I could not help having something to eat and drink at all the parties. On the seventeenth, there were a lot of parties with 23 in my class. Wow, there were a lot of treats.

My mom and dad gave all the kids invitations to my combination party on the 31st and just about everybody said they could come. I can't think of anybody who did not come because mine was the only class gathering that day.

On Sunday the 17th, I scheduled my visits to parties so that I would be in my own neighborhood about when it was going to get dark. I stopped home to tell mom and dad I was OK and then I went to two more parties on our street.

By the time I got home for good, I had eaten so much and drank so much soda, that my belly was aching a little. I told mom and dad I was OK. I meant that I was not ready to throw-up. I was close though! Before I knew it, I was asleep on the couch. When I woke up, it was time for bed and I was feeling pretty good.

The same bunch of boys and girls were at the parties on the 24th which was the Sunday before my Communion and Birthday Party. I was smart enough on this day not to overdo it on the sweets and soda so I was not sick at all when I got home.

I was getting excited knowing that it would be just one more week until I had my big party and that something great was supposed to happen about my wings.

Before I knew it, it was my birthday. I felt great. I felt something funny like as if I were stronger than I ever was. This was Thursday May 28. Dad and mom took all us kids to get a Dairy Queen Ice Cream. It was just a little car ride from the house.

Oh, yeah, before that, I almost forgot, mom and dad took us to McDonalds where we had cheese burgs and fries and an orange drink.

That was all great but there was nothing better than the Dairy Queen Ice Cream cone—a large for me. When I went up to bed on my birthday, Mortrock had already fallen asleep.

I shrugged my shoulders a couple times and it all seemed heavier and yet I felt stronger. Our two bedroom windows had big thick and high wooden awnings that dad had made. They were beautiful. There was a one foot little porch on the bottom of the awnings a little lower than window-sill height.

For years after he built them, I would sometimes sit on the little porch when nobody was looking. I knew it was dangerous but I held on to the sides real tight.

I think Dad put the little porch there for a flower box but he never built the flower-box. Humph!

The windows were low and tall and I could actually walk out onto the little porch no sweat—right from Mortrock's bedroom. I never hit my head on the awning. I was not tired at all after the birthday celebration. So, I figured: what the heck?

I was thinking that I might see if something had changed regarding my wings. I had only a few hours left before midnight. It was my seventh birthday. I had reached the age of reason.

Then, as I was going out the window onto the little porch, I felt something in my back under the shoulders. When I got out there, behind me I could feel the wings. They were there. I knew it. They had grown right through my pajamas.

There was no wind that early evening and it had just gotten dark—like it was dusk. I decided to flap my arms to see what would happen. When I flapped my arms a big wind or so it seemed came from under me. I hears a sound like "whoosh!" and I was no longer on the porch . I looked down and I could see the roof of our house on 54 Cummings Street.

"What the heck was that?" I thought. I found myself moving my arms which seemed to move my wings to keep me afloat in the air..

Then I knew. I was flying. It was effortless and for every move I decided to make in the sky, when I moved what I thought were my arms, my new wings would move me faster in the air. Was that something?

Something I soon noticed was that I did not crash into anything even though I had no built-in idea of how to avoid anything. It was as if I couldn't get hurt. When I came close to something like an antenna on a roof or a chimney, my wings seemed to have a mind of their own and they moved me in a direction where no harm could come to me. That was so neat!

It took a while before I got better and almost knew how to control where I was going. Yet, even when I felt confident, I was still a bit afraid and I still could not figure out how to land.

I remembered that Mr. Christian had asked me to come to his house when I was able to use my gifts (my wings) so I did. Glad I remembered.

As I approached his house, I was amazed. In the sky above me was what looked like a huge, possibly menacing bird. I had never seen such a large flying creature. I was magnetized by it as it seemed and I was already headed for it. What now?

As this huge flying object circled Mr. Christian's house, I was heading for a collision but I had not had one yet so maybe it would be OK?

Before long, this huge bird was right next to me. I mean it was flying right next to me. It began to talk. Its voice was the same voice as Mr. Christian. I looked over at the bird and sure enough, it actually was Mr. Christian with wings. He looked just like a huge angel.

He told me that he knew that I would be over and he was about to tell me how to land on his back deck—which did not have a roof. I listened intently and he had me make some moves and at one point, in our practice, we almost landed.

He then said we would go around one more time and he gave me a few more pointers about maneuvers that I should do and this time when we went around I did exactly what he had said.

Before I knew it, I was on his deck on my feet, and he was right next to me. There was no noise when we landed but I felt gravity keeping me on the deck. When my feet hit the deck, there was not even a "thud."

He then said, "watch this!" I saw what he did and then I saw his wings retract under his clothes and I could not see where they had been. He told me to do the same thing but I did not know what he had really done and I told him that.

He told me to just go ahead and do it and as soon as I thought about retracing my own wings, I felt them moving and in an instant they were under my clothing (pajamas at the time).

They seemed to go someplace inside of me which perhaps the angels had built for them. Once that happened I could not feel the presence of my wings anymore. They would come out again later when I had to leave to fly for home.

I had been thinking for years that Mr. Christian might be a wizard but just then, I began to think, after seeing him fly with his huge wings, that maybe he was an angel. Could that be? It was 1987 after all and maybe anything could happen.

Before anybody said anything, I asked Mr. Christian if he were an angel and without hesitation he said, "yes." We already knew secrets that nobody else knew then or still knows. He was truthful.

He was not a wizard but he had lots more power than what anybody would ever call a "wizard." I never followed Harry Potter but if there ever was a real Harry Potter like a real Brian P. Katille, perhaps he too had an angel.

He added that his mission from God and the heavenly hosts was to live with the people like as if he were a regular human. His job was to help as many people as much as he could.

He said that St. Peter had assigned me to him or him to me however you choose to see it. It was for light training. He informed me that for me it was all voluntary.

If I chose to end the gifts or did not want to help in the mission, it would end and I would forget about it completely. I told him I wanted to help.

He reminded me that there are no pictures of real angels anywhere on earth, but some people have doctored photographs that look very much like real angels when they materialize. Of course, humans with the gifts of wings and other angels could see them as they really are. Mr. Christian had looked amazing with his wings.

I wish I could show you all his beautiful wings as you read this chapter. What I can do, however, is show you what a younger Mr. Christian would look very much like, when bedecked with full wings.

Though this is not really Mr. Christian because he cannot be photographed, he looks a lot like this picture to me. Yes, he looks so much like this that I could probably be convinced that it was actually him. The rendering is on the very next page:

Photo very close to Mr. Christian's image taken inside of a parking facility

Mr. Christian had another name, an angel name that he explained to me but it was too long for me to remember and on this birthday night, I was too excited to pay attention to that part. I would ask him again someday. He did explain an awful lot that I remembered to me and he did it all in just fifteen minutes.

When he was finished instructing me, he said he had to go inside—back to his family. He told me when I went home, I should land on the little porch and go inside and go immediately to bed and to sleep. He said some more wonderful thoughts would be revealed to me this night as I was sleeping. They were.

After he went in, I went through everything he had told me about flying and landing and soon I was in the air again with my huge wings propelling me effortlessly in the sky. I could go anywhere just by thinking about doing it.

It was just like walking. When you decide to take a step and then you take the step, it just happens. It was amazing. Don't try any of this at home folks. It took me seven years to grow my wings.

I learned that I could adjust my speed and I could actually go so fast that I could become invisible. Mr. Christian confirmed this. I tried it and it worked. I don't know how to explain it but I could go so fast and yet stay still at the same time and when that happened, to the eyes of everybody including me, I became invisible.

I know that when I did that, I could not even see my own hand. Each time I repeated something that Mr. Christian had taught me, I got better at it. Like most things in life, my experience made me better at what I did. Soon I could fly without all the heavy thinking.

I figured I had a lot more to learn about this new business of being able to fly and how to tend to a new set of wings—even though I could not even see them. I was still amazed.

I also knew that right then, as I was daydreaming in the sky, that it was time to land. I began to think about landing and before I knew it, I was on the little porch under the awning outside of one of my brother Mortrock's bedroom windows. Again, like Mr. Christian had said; it was no sweat.

I did not plan to go out flying any more that night so as soon as I thought that thought, my wings retracted and I went in through the window and then I washed up and went right to bed.

I had been worrying about not fitting through the window but as it turns out, I did not have to worry. There was no dressing or undressing. I still had my pajamas on. I went to bed happily and I knew that in just a few days was the big party.

Chapter 16 Time for the Big Party

Mom baked all the cupcakes and I took this picture. Can't fine me!

I never saw so many people at our home except for mom's Easter Egg Hunt party in April or late March each year. These are most of the kids from First Communion Class and some neighbors and my cousins. There were lots more there than in this one picture.

Some were in different rooms before they sang Happy Birthday! Dad and mom were so happy about the First Communion and my birthday that they invited everybody they knew or so it seemed. The house was packed.

Some of the kids were relatives and some were neighbors and there were actually some kids at this great party that I did not even know. Of course my best swimming buddy, Mary Zabola and her older sisters Dawn and Kim, and her brother David were at the party with Mrs. Barbie Zabola and Mr. Joe Zabolo.

Mr. Zabola was with dad in our sunroom. They were good buddies. Aunt Diane and Uncle Joe and Uncle Ed were there and the two Pops as well as Uncle Marty & Aunt Cathy Scott & Lynn and Bucko & Barbara, Tobo Rodski, Al & Karen Komorek, Frannie & Joanne, Josh, as well as Mike K.and Cathy and others.

That room was situated under my new bedroom. It was built by dad, plus some uncles and friends and the pops when Katers was born. I never knew why the room had a soundproof floor until recently. Nobody would be able to sleep upstairs once one of dad and mom's parties got going. This was a really big one.

From the outside deck over the years, there was a door that looked like a closet. It originally was a closet until Dad built the Sunroom with my new bedroom on top of it. It became the one-room in the house in which the fine golden adult beverages would be swilled at exactly the same time as when the kids parties were going on outside and in the rest of the house.

Though after the addition was built, there was no more closet behind the door (It was what was called the sun room), it is true that as a little baby in the baby carrier, I spent the whole summer (my first) in that entrance area. It was nice and cool inside and I mean that in a lot of ways.

Now I know that dad had changed his choices over the years from a keg of Erlanger then to Harp Lager and then to Dortmunder Action Beer (DAB) and now I think dad's favorite keg is Stella Artois. Yes, I am proud of dad and now at my older age, I am proud of myself too. Dad always bought good beer.

What I remember most about my first birthday party at seven years of age (the age of reason) is that I understood almost all of the mystery by then or so it seemed.

After I fell asleep Thursday night (my birthday). I had Friday and Saturday nights—that was two more nights of surreptitious flying and successful landings as I was waiting for this great gathering. Besides having used these great gifts, the party was great. In fact, it was even better than my high expectations.

With all my buddies from the First Communion Class and lots others, I had one of the most magical days and nights ever.

I was so glad I did not have to visit anybody like on the 17th and all my good buds were here. I was also glad that mom and dad had invited so many people that even they did not know all who were coming.

Mom tallied it up afterwards and there were eighty-three people altogether at this great party. Thanks mom and dad.

They came to celebrate my birthday and My First Communion and I loved them all for that. At the time, I did not know where all the food and all the kids drinks came from though I knew where the keg came from. Funny! Nonetheless, the party was as good as it could be. Adults and children were all together when they sang:

> Happy Birthday to You
> Happy Birthday to You
> Happy Birthday Dear Brian
> Happy Birthday to You.
>
> Thank you everybody!

Let me tell you sincerely, it was not the words of the tune but that the people singing the tune really meant it and it was beautiful. It was the nicest birthday of all seven which God had given me to celebrate. I say to this day in earnest, I loved it. Thank you very much mom and dad, and all the wonderful people who helped me reach the age of reason.

Chapter 17 The Rest of My Life So Far

Some of my favorite spots to visit

To remind you, the two black & white photographs above were taken around sunset on different days. They are not pictures of me per se. However, they are photos of renditions—what a person with my gifts would look like if they were captured by camera.

I would have looked much like this from the age of seven to the age of twelve when my period with wings, as foretold by Mr. Christian was to end.

On May 29, the day after my birthday, I could not wait until dusk to do some more flying before the party.

There was a chill in the air but not cold enough to keep me out of the sky. I found myself going west and before long, I saw the Susquehanna River down by the Black Diamond in South Wilkes-Barre, PA. It was almost sundown and the sky was beautiful and the area around the river was outstanding to see.

The two photos on the prior page represent two fields that I encountered by the river. As you can see the first photograph shows "me" in a narrow meadow between trees. You can see how beautiful the greenery is and the trees and the look of the trees in the setting sun. Who would not want to be able to fly there?

If I were to have flown in the opposite direction, I would soon have reached a large corn field. It might have been Lucas' Farm.

The farmers would plant corn by the river as it was typically very rich soil from past flooding and because in an emergency, such as a dry summer, irrigation could be pumped in to give the plants a nice drink of water to continue their growth

In the second photo, you can see some large birds flying on the upper right side of the sky. When I had been up there before I landed in the greenery, I was flying with the birds and they treated me like I was just another bird. I loved it!

Though in that area of the river there is a major population center of neighborhoods, somebody seemed to be shooting at the geese. I wondered at the time but later when I talked to Mr. Christian, he told me that I was invisible to hunters and nobody would ever be shooting at me.

While I was with the geese, one of them was hit by a piece of shotgun pellot and went to the ground by the big open area shown in the second picture. I flew down as the goose was about to hit the ground and I caught it and held it under my wing. I was amazed at what I then saw. God is great!

The goose and I were communicating but not in English, my language. I understood what he was saying. He had been wounded in one of his wings. As we landed, I saw the wound get smaller and smaller until it actually was gone.

The goose stayed with me a while as if to say thank-you and then when he felt ready, he flew off to meet the other geese who were still flying above.

The shooting stopped and I saw some dogs in the area looking for the fallen goose. Obviously they did not find him. He had been healed and was back in the sky.

Later when I spoke with Mr. Christian, he told me that my wings had special powers and could promote the healing of any wounded creature—animal or human.

He said he was sorry that he had not told me about that but things happened the way they should have. He agreed that there was communication between the goose and I but not the normal way humans communicate.

He told me that was part of my mission when flying. I was to watch out for animals and humans who were in peril and when possible I was to fly to go save them, take them home, rescue them from predicaments or whatever I could do to help.

He congratulated me on my first episode with the goose and assured me there would be plenty more as I led my five year period with the great gifts

Close out the book now, Brian?

Before I close out this book, as for the most part, I have told the story of my magical wings and the great angel, Mr. Christian. Now, please let me report on an event and then tell you just one more story that showed me just how important my gift was to all, including a member of my own family.

Chapter 18 What is Wrong with Brian?

Let me take you to July 22, 1987, almost two months after my birthday. Our family had just gotten back from Ocean City Md (above) where we had vacationed for almost a week. It was my dad's Sister Nancy's birthday and she celebrated with her Flanders family up in the East End section of Wilkes-Barre. Dad took me there and wished her happy birthday; gave her some tomatoes, and slipped her a small monetary gift that made her smile. I was with him and it was nice.

It was in the 90's—almost 95 degrees out and humid. Mortrock and I went swimming after I got home for most of the day. Mary Zabola was with us as was her sister Dawn. We got tired with all the laps and the sun beating down on us. Before dusk, Mortrock wanted to go upstairs and either nap or go to bed for the night. By the time I got upstairs, he was asleep or so it seemed. His room was so big, we hung out there a lot.

Dad did not like us boys going around the house without shirts so, to please dad, we almost always had our t-shirts on except when we were out swimming. When I got up to the room, I thought Mortrock was already cutting big ZZZZ's.

I did not have a summer t-shirt on because I had been swimming. I went out the window onto the little porch under the awning to get some air. I was about to sneak out for a quick flight to cool off when I heard Mortrock scream out, "Brian are you OK, what's wrong with your back. Brian, please come in now."

What had happened was my wings were on their way out so I could fly and Mortrock saw them and it looked to him like my back was all cut up. He was scared for his big brother. My wings immediately retracted.

He told me this when I came in. I showed him my back and he said he saw something that then disappeared. He was frightened and called for mom and dad. Katers was already asleep. Mom and dad arrived in what was like an instant.

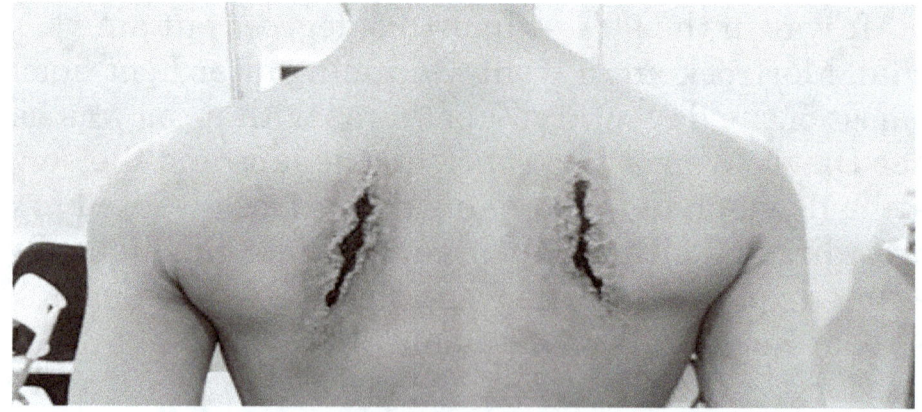

Though the above is not a picture of my back, it is very representative of what my brother saw when I was about to take off and fly. I can understand why he was so frightened.

Mortrock told his story about what he saw as huge sores on my back. He had no idea why my back looked like that for just an instant. He also told mom and dad that while he was looking at the marks, somehow they disappeared, which made him even more frightened. He felt he had seen something bad.

Of course, for years, mom and dad already knew about my gifts. However, my brother, Mortrock had never been told. Until this day, the secret had been safe.

Dad told mom that it was about time we tell my baby brother about my wonderful gifts. Mom did the talking in her soft voice and Mortrock said that he had some dreams about something like what she said but figured they were just dreams. My brother was OK and mom and dad went back downstairs,.

My brother and I spent hours talking after that and I told him everything about what happened to me five years earlier and then what had happened two months prior on my birthday when I took my first flight.

Mortrock's eyes were about the size of plums and bright as can be as I told him about the story of the gifts and about who Mr. Christian actually was. He was happy for me and he was amazed. I was glad he now knew.

Where's Pop Trosk?

Life went on as normal for the next couple years except for one thing. Eventually mom told Katers about me and she too was amazed and so I had to tell her all about everything, including Mr. Christian, my angel.

I was getting older and was about six months away from turning twelve when the family had a big scare.

We were all up Pop Trosk's house on Christmas Eve as we do every year. Aunt Sue was always the last to arrive with Matt and Alie, their two little guys. Uncle Mitch was there too. He drove them from Boston.

Sometimes Pop Trosk would come in later before we exchanged gifts and then he would sing Silent Night.

Nana "Skippo" Trosk finally admitted that she had not heard from Poppy and that is not like him. She called the Legion and he was not there and then she called Tommy Benson, his best buddy besides Joe Evans and he was not there either.

Everybody became worried about Pop Trosk. Nobody had any ideas.

Dad had been with Pop earlier in the day at the Republics Club annual Christmas Eve celebration. Dad told everybody that he had dropped Pop Trosk off at his house on Hillside Street and he saw him go in.

Nana remembered Pop freshening up in the downstairs bathroom sink and then going out again to see his buddies. He wished them Merry Christmas (Eve) every year on this day. The Trosks did not know anything about my special gifts.

Nana was almost crying. I knew she was very worried. When nobody was looking, I put my coat on and snuck out the back door.

Pop had taken me to the Legion enough times that I knew how to get there. I thought about flying to the Legion and sure enough my wings came through my coat and were all ready to go. I took off for the Legion.

It was a quick ride for me but it was dark out so I could not see well without coming down low. I went to where Pop normally parked but his car was not there.

Since it was Christmas Eve, I thought I would look all around wherever there were cars parked. Pop's car was dark and it blended in with the surroundings. On my second time around, I saw Pop Trosk's car in a remote area of a parking lot and I went to it.

I landed behind his car and I heard Pop asking, "Who's there?". I was glad he was conscious. It had been snowing and when Pop tried to get to his car, he slipped on the ice and I think he broke something. I had to get him to the hospital quickly.

After a couple years with my gifts, and my many encounters with Mr. Christian, I could now communicate my thoughts over distances to Mr. Christian. That saved us.

I asked Mr. C. to call Mr. Tommy Benson and ask him to put his coat on and come outside into his back yard and ask no questions.

I had never lifted so much weight but I knew inside I could do it. I used my left arm to lift Pop off the ground and I flew to Tommy Benson's house and I picked Tommy up with my right arm.

Tommy did not know what just happened but Pop told him as we flew. I had a good grip on both and I was still able to fly.

I made it to the General Hospital Emergency room in less than five minutes. For me, there was no traffic. I put Pop Trosk on a bench and I walked Tommy to the entrance. I had explained to Tommy on the way what he needed to do.

Mr. Christian had already called the Hospital and so when Tommy approached the entrance, the EMTs were there to meet him and he quickly took them to the bench where Pop was resting.

I had retracted my wings so nobody would know how Pop had gotten to the hospital. They put Pop on a gurney and quickly took him inside to the main ER room. There was no delay.

Tommy Benson was not permitted in the treatment room . After he gave the information, he called Nana and told her he had taken Pop Trosk to the hospital and that he was going go be all right.

Nana called out to everybody at Pop's house that Pop was OK. Tommy then told her that Pop needed a Christmas morning operation. He explained it all to Nana while I was flying back to the Trosk house. Somehow, I was able to sneak back into the house without anybody knowing I had been gone. Everybody was so worried about Poppy that nobody was thinking right. I was unnoticed.

I went in and then quickly came out of the downstairs bathroom. Nobody knew. When I came out of the bathroom, they told me that Pop was OK and that he had an accident and thank God Tommy Benson had saved him. Dad knew I was gone but he did not let on and later we discussed what had happened. He was very proud of me. I said nothing.

Tommy Benson taking Pop Piotroski to the hospital made Nana Skippo and all my Trosk uncles & aunts feel much better. In fact, we all felt really good knowing that not all such stories end well.

So, in honor of Pop we all sang Silent Night and then as we did every year, we opened the gifts. Of course, Breezie already had his three squeak toys from Pop opened before any gifts were exchanged.

The sound of the squeaks from Pop's favorite doggie's toys helped everybody's face put on a big Christmas smile.

After the holidays, Dad told mom and Mortrock and Katers what had happened; but to this day, Pop Trosk thanks Tommy Benson for the whole thing. I love it.

The funniest thing is that Tommy Benson himself still cannot remember how he was the hero and he is still puzzled about where he left his car at the hospital.

He remembers that after he got a ride home by a hospital employee, the next day his car was in front of his house like it always was.

He blamed it on a bit too much Christmas Cheer but was glad to have helped. Funny how these great gifts work. Something tells me, however, Mr. Christian was doing a lot of work behind the scenes.

When Katers, Mortrock and I got up the next morning, which was Christmas day, we learned that Pop Trosk had broken his hip. His favorite surgeon was Dr. Sanford Sternlieb and he had come in the hospital to fix Poppy. Thank God, this major operation was a success.

Pop Trosk was in the hospital on Christmas Day so we hoped to see him. After we opened our gifts from Santa, Dad and Pop Katille, and Grandma Biddie, mom, Katers, Mortrock, and I went to see him in the hospital. He was already chipper.

He said it all went pretty quickly. His pain was so severe they gave him pain killers which knocked him out. He said he had a dream about being hurt and that a big bird flew him to the hospital. He had no idea…

He admitted to us at the Hospital that he had enjoyed his share of cheer at the Legion and so he figured the big bird notion was a very imaginative dream that was helped along by a very important person, Lord Calvert.

Pop was in the hospital for a week to make sure all the bones in his hip area would set properly. When he got all better, his hip, which had been broken once before when he was in his twenties, was actually about 100% better than it was before his first accident.

Pop thanked God for all the Lord did to help. But, somehow, he is still having dreams about being in the arms of this big bird. Maybe if Mr. Christian permits it, I will tell him what happened one day but I do not want to diminish the role Tommy Benson had. I sometimes wonder what if Tommy Benson would not go along with such an unusual request for a favor/

Mr. Christian and little Billie

I was eleven years old at the time, and I would be twelve in May and that was supposed to end my ability to fly as my gifts were temporary and I knew they were.

After Poppy was well on the mend, I wanted to personally thank Mr. Christian, my personal angel for the help he gave me in so many ways to help save Pop Trosk. So I walked to his house and I rang the bell.

Mrs. Christian answered the door and invited me in. She poured me a glass of milk and gave me some cookies. Meanwhile Mr. Christian was upstairs with little Billie. Soon, they came down and we all sat at the dining room table.

Mr. Christian had never told me that little Billie had been given the gifts that I received but he did on this day. We all, those of us at the table, knew what that meant. He thanked me for my good work with the gifts. He highlighted what he called "my great effort" with Pop Trosk.

He told me that if by chance I took the time to ask him about flying two grown men to the hospital as an eleven year old, he would have said that at my age I should not have been able to lift both men at all and surely would not be able to fly them to the hospital. He asked me how much I loved Pop Trosk. I opened my arms as wide as I could and he got the message.

He said that in addition to the gifts I had been given, that the big gift of love was in play as in all scenarios of life, and it was love that helped me to carry the huge load to the hospital.

He said that nobody of which he knew had ever done that before. Ever. He said his angel friends were impressed that love could be so powerful and strong to enable a human—even with wings, to carry the day.

We talked about my years with the gifts and he told me that Billie's shoulders were getting more muscular and that he would be ready soon just like I became ready as I turned seven years old, the age of reason. He then surprised me when he asked if there were anything that would make me wish to keep the gifts.

I immediately said "yes. just tell me that I can." He said, "you can...done!" He added that if things change, he would talk to me about that but he was very happy that I had said, "yes." He asked me if I would help with little Billie's training and I told him I would be proud to do so. What an honor!

Even if this story were not about me, Brian Patrick Katille, I would have been pleased to tell the story to you all. Thank you sincerely for reading it.

And that my friends wraps up my story about the Christmas Wings for Brian (Me). I hope you liked it. Now that I am back on duty, working for the Christian Force, please do not be afraid if one day when you look up in the sky you see a big bird that looks like he has human legs and he is wearing sneakers. Just say "Hello," and I would be pleased to say "Hello" right back atcha!

Isn't life great?
God bless you all & Merry Christmas!

Other Books by Brian W. Kelly: (amazon.com, and Kindle)

The Cowardly Congress Whatever happened to Congress doing the work of the people?
Help for Mayor George and Next Mayor of Wilkes-Barre How to vote for the next Mayor Council abbreviated
Ghost of Wilkes-Barre Future: Spirit's advice for residents about how to pick the next Mayor and Council
Great Players in Air Force Football: Air Force's best players of all time
Great Coaches in Air Force Football: From Coach 1 to Coach Troy Calhoun
Great Moments in Air Force Football: From day 1 to today
Great Players in Navy Football: Navy's best including Bellino & Staubach
Great Coaches in Navy Football: From Coach 1 to Coach #39 Ken Niumatalolo
Great Moments in Navy Football: From day 1 to coach Ken Niumatalolo l
No Tree! No Toys! No Toot! Heartwarming story. Christmas gone while 19 month old napped
How to End DACA, Sanctuary Cities, & Resident Illegal Aliens , best solution to wipe shadows in America.
Government Must Stop Ripping Off Seniors' Social Security!: Hey buddy, seniors can no longer spare a dime?
Special Report: Solving America's Student Debt Crisis!: The only real solution to the $1.52 Trillion debt
How to End DACA, Sanctuary Cities, & Resident Illegal Aliens , best solution to wipe shadows in America.
The Winning Political Platform for America Unique winning approach to solve the big problems in America.
Lou Barletta v Bob Casey for US Senate Barletta's unique approach to solving the big problems in America.
John Chrin v Matt Cartwright for Congress Chrin has a unique approach to solving big problems in America.
The Cure for Hate !!! Can the cure be any worse than this disease that is crippling America?
Andrew Cuomo's Time to Go? "He Was Never that Great!": Cuomo says America never that great
White People Are Bad! Bad! Bad! Whoever thought a popular slogan in 2018 would be It's OK to be White!
The Fake News Media Is Also Corrupt !!!: Fake press / media today is not worthy to be 4th Estate.
God Gave US Donald Trump?   Trump was sent from God as the people's answer
Millennials Say America Was "Never That Great": Too many pleased days of political chumps not over!
White People Are Bad! Bad! Bad! In 2018, too many people find race as a non-equalizer.
It's Time for The John Q. Doe Party… Don't you think? By Elephants.
Great Players in Florida Gators Football… Tim Tebow and a ton of other great players
Great Coaches in Florida Gators Football… The best coaches in Gator history.
The Constitution by Hamilton, Jefferson, Madison, et al. The Real Constitution
The Constitution Companion. Will help you learn and understand the Constitution
Great Coaches in Clemson Football The best Clemson Coaches right to Dabo Swinney
Great Players in Clemson Football The best Clemson players in history
Winning Back America. America's been stolen and can be won back completely
The Founding of America… Great book to pick up a lot of great facts
Defeating America's Career Politicians. The scoundrels need to go.
Midnight Mass by Jack Lammers… You remember what it was like Great story
The Bike by Jack Lammers… Great heartwarming Story by Jack
Wipe Out All Student Loan Debt--Now! Watch the economy go boom!
No Free Lunch Pay Back Welfare! Why not pay it back?
Deport All Millennials Now!!! Why they deserve to be deported and/or saved
DELETE the EPA, Please! The worst decisions to hurt America
Taxation Without Representation 4th Edition Should we throw the TEA overboard again?
Four Great Political Essays by Thomas Dawson
Top Ten Political Books for 2018… Cliffnotes Version of 10 Political Books
Top Six Patriotic Books for 2018… Cliffnotes version of 6 Patriotic Boosk
Why Trump Got Elected!.. It's great to hear about a great milestone in America!
The Day the Free Press Died. Corrupt Press Lives on!
Solved (Immigration) The best solutions for 2018
Solved II (Obamacare, Social Security, Student Debt) Check it out; They're solved.
Great Moments in Pittsburgh Steelers Football... Six Super Bowls and more.
Great Players in Pittsburgh Steelers Football ,,,Chuck Noll, Bill Cowher, Mike Tomin, etc.
Great Coaches in New England Patriots Football,,, Bill Belichick the one and only plus others
Great Players in New England Patriots Football… Tom Brady, Drew Bledsoe et al.
Great Coaches in Philadelphia Eagles Football..Andy Reid, Doug Pederson & Lots more
Great Players in Philadelphia Eagles Football Great players such as Sonny Jurgenson
Great Coaches in Syracuse Football All the greats including Ben Schwartzwalder
Great Players in Syracuse Football. Highlights best players such as Jim Brown & Donovan McNabb
Millennials are People Too !!! Give US millennials help to live American Dream
Brian Kelly for the United States Senate from PA: Fresh Face for US Senate
The Candidate's Bible. Don't pray for your campaign without this bible
Rush Limbaugh's Platform for Americans… Rush will love it
Sean Hannity's Platform for Americans… Sean will love it
Donald Trump's New Platform for Americans. Make Trump unbeatable in 2020
Tariffs Are Good for America! One of the best tools a president can have
Great Coaches in Pittsburgh Steelers Football Sixteen of the best coaches ever to coach in pro football.
Great Moments in New England Patriots Football Great football moments from Boston to New England

Great Moments in Philadelphia Eagles Football. The best from the Eagles from the beginning of football.
Great Moments in Syracuse Football The great moments, coaches & players in Syracuse Football
Boost Social Security Now! Hey Buddy Can You Spare a Dime?
The Birth of American Football. From the first college game in 1869 to the last Super Bowl
Obamacare: A One-Line Repeal Congress must get this done.
A Wilkes-Barre Christmas Story A wonderful town makes Christmas all the better
A Boy, A Bike, A Train, and a Christmas Miracle A Christmas story that will melt your heart
Pay-to-Go   America-First Immigration Fix
Legalizing Illegal Aliens Via Resident Visas Americans-first plan saves $Trillions. Learn how!
60 Million Illegal Aliens in America!!! A simple, America-first solution.
The Bill of Rights By Founder James Madison Refresh your knowledge of the specific rights for all
Great Players in Army Football Great Army Football played by great players..
Great Coaches in Army Football Army's coaches are all great.
Great Moments in Army Football Army Football at its best.
Great Moments in Florida Gators Football Gators Football from the start. This is the book.
Great Moments in Clemson Football CU Football at its best. This is the book.
Great Moments in Florida Gators Football Gators Football from the start. This is the book.
The Constitution Companion. A Guide to Reading and Comprehending the Constitution
The Constitution by Hamilton, Jefferson, & Madison − Big type and in English
PATERNO: The Dark Days After Win # 409. Sky began to fall within days of win # 409.
JoePa 409 Victories: Say No More! Winningest Division I-A football coach ever
American College Football: The Beginning From before day one football was played.
Great Coaches in Alabama Football Challenging the coaches of every other program!
Great Coaches in Penn State Football the Best Coaches in PSU's football program
Great Players in Penn State Football The best players in PSU's football program
Great Players in Notre Dame Football The best players in ND's football program
Great Coaches in Notre Dame Football The best coaches in any football program
Great Players in Alabama Football from Quarterbacks to offensive Linemen Greats!
Great Moments in Alabama Football AU Football from the start. This is the book.
Great Moments in Penn State Football PSU Football, start--games, coaches, players,
Great Moments in Notre Dame Football ND Football, start, games, coaches, players
Cross Country with the Parents A great trip from East Coast to West with the kids
Seniors, Social Security & the Minimum Wage. Things seniors need to know.
How to Write Your First Book and Publish It with CreateSpace. You too can be an author.
The US Immigration Fix--It's all in here. Finally, an answer.
I had a Dream IBM Could be #1 Again The title is self-explanatory
WineDiets.Com Presents The Wine Diet Learn how to lose weight while having fun.
Wilkes-Barre, PA; Return to Glory Wilkes-Barre City's return to glory
Geoffrey Parsons' Epoch... The Land of Fair Play Better than the original.
The Bill of Rights 4 Dummmies! This is the best book to learn about your rights.
Sol Bloom's Epoch ...Story of the Constitution The best book to learn the Constitution
America 4 Dummmies! All Americans should read to learn about this great country.
The Electoral College 4 Dummmies! How does it really work?
The All-Everything Machine Story about IBM's finest computer server.
ThankYou IBM! This book explains how IBM was beaten in the computer marketplace by neophytes

Amazon.com/author/brianwkelly
Brian W. Kelly has written 217 books including this one.
Thank you for buying this one.
Others can be found at amazon.com/author/brianwkelly

www.ingramcontent.com/pod-product-compliance
Lightning Source LLC
Chambersburg PA
CBHW070520260626
47161CB00004B/1598